"I thought it was just a little bump."

"It is. It's just a bloody one." He applied some antibiotic ointment to the small scrape, trying to ignore the way her soft, lightly floral perfume was making his blood run hot.

He'd never been a man prone to indulging his every sexual whim, but this particular dose of desire was taking a toll on his legendary self-control.

He backed away, giving himself room to breathe. "I think the bleeding's stopped now."

She turned to face him. "Thanks."

Something intriguing glittered in her eyes. Nix knew it would be folly to speculate what that intriguing something might be. But he'd never been any good at turning his back on a puzzle. Especially one that smelled like wildflowers.

THE SECRET OF CHEROKEE COVE

PAULA GRAVES

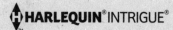

Recycling programs
for this product may
not exist in your area.

For my #1k1hr pals on Twitter. Y'all make writing
on deadline fun. Okay, maybe not fun, but
definitely bearable. Keep #writing!

ISBN-13: 978-0-373-74800-6

THE SECRET OF CHEROKEE COVE

Copyright © 2014 by Paula Graves

Printed in U.S.A.

www.Harlequin.com

ABOUT THE AUTHOR

Alabama native Paula Graves wrote her first book, a mystery starring herself and her neighborhood friends, at the age of six. A voracious reader, Paula loves books that pair tantalizing mystery with compelling romance. When she's not reading or writing, she works as a creative director for a Birmingham advertising agency and spends time with her family and friends. She is a member of Southern Magic Romance Writers, Heart of Dixie Romance Writers and Romance Writers of America.

Paula invites readers to visit her website, www.paulagraves.com.

Books by Paula Graves

HARLEQUIN INTRIGUE

*Cooper Justice
**Cooper Justice: Cold Case Investigation
§Cooper Security
‡‡Bitterwood P.D.

CAST OF CHARACTERS

Dana Massey—In Bitterwood for her brother's engagement party, it's his suspicious car crash that keeps the deputy U.S. marshal in town, where she stumbles onto a cold case with very personal implications.

Walker Nix—The Bitterwood P.D. detective knows it's a bad idea for Dana to get involved in the investigation, but as the case takes a series of unexpected turns, she may be the perfect person to have on his side.

Doyle Massey—The Bitterwood chief of police has made enemies in his short time at the head of the police force. Has his investigation into police corruption made him a target? Or is the motive more personal?

Laney Hanvey—Doyle's fiancée will do what it takes to make sure her groom stays alive for the wedding. Could she know something about the attempt on Doyle's life and not even realize it?

Pete Sutherland—The town's most popular citizen is both rich and well respected. So why does his name keep showing up in the middle of the investigation?

Briar Blackwood—Bitterwood's night shift dispatcher knows a few secrets about Dana's mother. Could the crazy story she tells be the truth?

Derek Albertson—The former chief of police comes under attack for talking to Nix. But why? What does he know that he's not telling?

Alvin Pitts—The retired cop helped Doyle and Dana's mother leave Bitterwood when she was a young, scared teenager. Does he know the decades-old secret she was keeping?

Paul and Nina Hale—The wealthy pair crossed paths with Dana's mother over thirty years ago. So why aren't they willing to talk to Dana now?

Chapter One

She entered the Bitterwood Community Center banquet hall with no fanfare, a tall, fit woman in her early thirties. Fanfare or not, Walker Nix found his gaze drawn her way, taking in her appearance with the practiced eye of an investigator. She had sleek auburn hair worn straight and intelligent green eyes that scanned the room with a specific goal in mind, narrowing as she failed to find her target.

I should paint her, he thought. She wasn't pretty, exactly, but he found her striking features interesting.

Conversation died to nothing as most of the partygoers turned to look at the newcomer. Laney Hanvey, standing near the front of the hall with her mother and sister, crossed quickly to the woman, a smile on her face. She passed Walker, leaving him with a whiff of her light jasmine scent, and extended her hand to the taller woman.

"Dana. You look just like your photo. It's so nice to finally meet you!"

Chief's sister, Nix thought, his interest tempered by the impracticality of lusting after a woman whose brother was his boss. Her impending arrival had been the talk of the police station from the time the chief had mentioned to one of the file clerks that she was coming. She'd be in town only a few days, just long enough to get to know her brother's fiancée and catch up on their lives, before heading back to her job in Atlanta.

Still, his gaze lingered on Dana Massey's face as she smiled at Laney and took her hand with what appeared to be genuine pleasure. She really would be a fascinating subject to paint.

"I'm so happy to finally meet you, Laney!" Dana maintained eye contact as if oblivious to the interested stares of everyone else in the room. Nix dragged his gaze away from the meeting of the future sisters-in-law and let it skim across the other faces in the hall. To his surprise, he saw several looks of shock and one or two expressions of near hostility.

Odd, he thought. As far as he knew, this was Dana Massey's first visit to Bitterwood. And what little he'd heard about her wouldn't elicit hostility from anyone but the fugitives she chased in her job as a deputy U.S. marshal.

"Doyle is late," Laney was saying as she and

Dana passed Nix's position near the doorway. "I tried calling his phone, but he's not answering."

"He's probably lost it somewhere," Dana murmured in the tone of a sister used to her younger brother's foibles. "He loses a phone every year, I swear."

They passed out of earshot, and Nix made himself look at his watch, not Dana Massey's shapely backside. Almost eight. The party had officially started at seven-thirty. And while Bitterwood chief of police Doyle Massey had a reputation for being a bit more laid-back than his predecessor, he'd never shown a tendency toward tardiness.

Nix bumped gazes with one of his fellow detectives, small, dark-eyed Ivy Calhoun. She was newly married, tanned golden from her recent honeymoon in the Bahamas and looking happier than he'd ever seen her. She flashed a smile at him, and he wandered over to where she stood with her new husband, Sutton Calhoun.

"Nix." Sutton greeted him with a nod. They were both Bitterwood natives, but Sutton was a few years younger than Nix. He was better acquainted with Nix's younger brother, Lavelle, which might explain the wariness in Sutton's gaze. Lavelle had never been anything but trouble.

"Calhoun," Nix responded in kind, saving his

smile for Sutton's bride. "Have you heard from the chief?"

Ivy shook her head. "Laney said he told her he had to pick up something from the office before he came to the party. But that was nearly an hour ago."

It didn't take an hour to get anywhere in Bitterwood. "Have you tried calling the station to see if he showed up?"

Ivy cocked her head slightly to one side, her gaze narrowing. "You think something's wrong?"

"One of your hunches?" Sutton added, not without a hint of sarcasm.

"No," Nix lied, even though his hunch meter was going off like a klaxon. "Just doesn't seem much like the chief to keep his girl waiting."

"Is that his sister?" Ivy nodded toward Dana Massey, who stood at the front talking to Laney and her family.

"Yes," Nix answered. "She didn't seem worried about her brother's lateness."

Sutton took a sip from the cup of red punch he held in his right hand. With a grimace, he set the cup on a nearby table. "Maybe she knows stuff about him we don't."

"Maybe," Nix conceded.

"But you don't think so," Ivy prodded.

He gave her a warning look, but her eyebrows

merely rose a notch and her dark eyes flashed with amusement.

She thought it was all great fun, having a genuine Cherokee soothsayer on the police force, and most of the time Nix didn't try to squelch her enjoyment. He wasn't a soothsayer, of course—his hunches were usually based on deduction, not intuition. And he was only part Cherokee. The rest was pure Appalachian Scots-Irish, as his brother Lavelle's headstrong ways would attest. But playing the inscrutable Indian could have its advantages, especially during interrogations.

"I'll give the station a call, see what's what." He wandered away and pulled out his cell phone to call the main switchboard.

The night shift dispatcher, Briar Blackwood, answered, "Bitterwood P.D."

"Hey, Briar, it's Nix. Have you seen the chief?"

"He called about seven to say he was heading in to pick something up from his office, but he didn't show. I figured he might have been running late and decided to come by after the party."

Nix frowned. "Yeah, that's probably it."

"What's wrong?" Briar asked.

"Probably nothing."

"Nix—"

"Later, Briar." He hung up before she could ask any more questions he couldn't answer and crossed back to where Ivy and Sutton stood, talking to a tall redhead and an even taller man with dark hair and a rangy but powerful build.

Ivy introduced the pair as Natalie and J. D. Cooper, friends of the chief's. "Natalie used to work with the chief down South," Ivy added as Nix shook hands.

Natalie smiled, but he saw concern hovering behind her green eyes. "Ivy says Doyle's late. Doyle's never late. He may come across as an overgrown frat boy sometimes, but he's as dependable as they come."

Her alarm exacerbated his own growing concern. Keeping his voice low, he told them about his call to the station. "That was an hour ago."

Ivy looked from Natalie's face back to Nix's. "Should we go look for him?"

"I'll do it," Nix volunteered. "You stay here and make sure Laney doesn't start worrying too much until we know what's what."

Unspoken between them was the fact that there might well be a damned good reason to worry. Only three months earlier, Doyle Massey had crossed swords with a man named Merritt Cortland, whose thirst for power had led him to kill his father and several others in a deadly explosion. He'd tried to make the chief another of his victims, but Massey had fought him off. After Cortland had fallen down a steep incline, landing on the rocks below, he'd been thought dead, but by the time paramedics arrived at the base of the bluff, his body was gone.

Was Merritt Cortland still alive? It was a question that nobody had been able to answer to anyone's satisfaction. Nix figured it was possible the man's injuries weren't fatal as the chief had assumed. It was equally possible that one of Cortland's ragtag cohort of meth cookers, anarchists and radical militia soldiers had recovered the body and was keeping it on ice in order to keep the legend alive.

Under Merritt Cortland's father, Wayne, the criminal operation had flourished, and even Cortland the younger had somehow managed to keep the enterprise afloat, despite the disparate elements involved. But if Merritt Cortland was dead, how long would the conspiracy thrive?

Outside the community center, night had fallen deep and blue. After a mild day, the temperature had dropped into the forties, driving Nix deeper into his leather jacket. As he started down the concrete steps to the sidewalk, the door opened behind him and footsteps clicked across the hard surface.

"Are you going to look for Doyle?"

The low female voice rippled along his nerves as if she'd run a finger down his spine. He turned to find Dana Massey standing on the steps behind him, her intelligent eyes full of stubborn intent.

Lying would do no good. She seemed like the

kind of woman who never asked a question if she didn't already know the answer. "I thought I'd see what's keeping him."

"How late is he?"

"Party started at seven-thirty, so—"

"When was the last time anyone heard from him?" She walked down the steps until she stood level with Nix, her head only a couple of inches below his own. She was as tall as her brother and had the same sort of dynamic presence, though the chief's aura of command was often tempered by his good-natured humor.

There was no humor in Dana Massey's green eyes at the moment.

"He called the police station around seven and told the dispatcher he was going to drop by the office before the party to pick up something."

"Pick up what?"

"Don't know."

Her lips flattened with annoyance, though her irritation didn't seem to be directed toward him. "Was he at home when he called?"

"Don't know that, either," he admitted. He should have asked the question of Briar, though the chief might not have said where he was. "I'm working on that assumption."

To her credit, she didn't make the usual joke about assumptions. "He's not answering his phone."

"So I hear."

She extended her hand suddenly, as if she'd just remembered they hadn't met. "Dana Massey. The chief's sister."

"Walker Nix. The chief's detective."

Her lips curved slightly at his dry rejoinder as she shook his hand. She had a firm, dry grip, with long fingers that felt like warm velvet against his own. "So I heard. Mind if I tag along?"

He could still feel the lingering sensation of her skin against his when he dropped her hand. "Wouldn't you rather stick around the party?"

She shook her head. "I'm here for my brother. Wherever he is."

He nodded toward the sidewalk. "Bundle up. My heater's acting up."

DANA EYED THE rusty-looking Ford pickup truck parked a block down Main Street from the community center, then shifted her gaze back to the tall, dark-eyed man who seemed to be watching her for her reaction. She got the feeling this moment was some sort of test, but damned if she knew what the right answer might be.

"Nice wheels," she murmured.

The right corner of his mouth quirked upward. "Thanks." He opened the passenger door without producing a key.

Her high heels weren't the most practical footwear for climbing into an oversized truck, but she managed to haul herself into the cab without making too much of a spectacle. Her wool slacks and cable-knit sweater had seemed to be sufficient for the cool night, but the truck's hard vinyl seat felt like a block of ice under her backside. She stifled a shiver and held her breath until she located the seat belt and reassured herself that it actually worked.

Walker Nix slid behind the steering wheel and engaged his own seat belt before turning to look at her. "Need a blanket?"

She bit back a shiver and shook her head no. "How far away is Doyle's house?"

"You're not staying there?"

She shook her head again, hoping he didn't ask any uncomfortable questions. "I booked a room at a motel in a town north of here. Quaint name—Purgatory."

"That's a bit of a drive."

A bit of a drive? Purgatory was maybe ten minutes away by car. A commute that short in Atlanta, where she lived and worked, was something to be deeply coveted.

Thinking of the short drive from Purgatory reminded her that her car was parked across the street. The Chevy featured soft seats and a working heater. But before she could suggest they take her car, Nix had already cranked the truck and swung it out of its parking place.

"You didn't see anything on the drive here?" Nix asked her.

"No, but I was already in town by seven." She'd waffled over the gift she'd picked out for her brother and his new bride on the drive from Atlanta and had decided to do some last-minute shopping in Bitterwood. But, of course, most of the town's quaint little shops had closed down at five. "Thought I'd do some last-minute shopping, but nothing was open."

"Everything closes at five around here."

"Everything?"

"Well, there are some joints here and there where you can paint the town red until you can't see straight. But I don't think they're selling what you were wanting to buy."

Like most of the other people she'd met since arriving in town, Walker Nix had a hard-edged mountain accent, though his was tempered a bit, as if he'd spent some time away from the hills. He wasn't handsome, exactly, but she rather liked the flat planes and hard angles of his features. He had olive skin and dark hair worn very short on the sides and only a little longer on top. Military-style, she guessed. Probably had some armed-forces service in his background—marine corps, or maybe army. Infantry, not rear echelon. The

man had jumped right to action at the first sign
of trouble.

Once they left the small town center, artificial lighting nearly disappeared, save for the oc-
casional residences spaced every few hundred
yards along the winding two-lane road. So the
sudden bright beams of light that split the darkness around a blind curve caught them both by
surprise. Nix hit the brakes, the sudden deceler-
ation slamming Dana hard against the restraint
belt crossing her chest. The brakes squealed, but
the truck shimmied to a stop a dozen yards short
of the large black truck that lay on its side in the
middle of the road, its headlights slicing through
the darkness.

*No, God, no. S*he stared at the wreck with a
knot in her gut. *Not Doyle, too.*

Before Dana could unlatch her seat belt, Nix
had jerked the truck in Park and jumped out, running toward the wreck. She joined him, cursing
the high heels that kept getting caught in the un-
even, rutted pavement. Terror sucked the air right
out of her lungs as she faltered to a stop in front
of the vehicle.

The beam of Nix's flashlight scanned across
the bloodied features of her brother Doyle.

Oh, God, please no.

Her brother's eyes opened, squinting against
the flashlight beam. She felt her knees wobble

and grabbed the first thing she could wrap her hand around—Nix's arm. "Doyle?"

Her brother's gaze met hers, and he forced a smile that looked more like a grimace. "About time you got here. I'm an hour late for my own engagement party, and nobody thinks to come looking for me?"

She nearly drooped with relief, dropping her hand from Nix's arm. Doyle sounded as if he was in pain, but his sense of humor was still in play. That had to be a good sign, right?

"How bad are you hurt?" Nix asked, shining the light toward the floor of the cab. Dana could see that one of Doyle's legs was broken. Grimacing, she looked back at his face, trying to figure out where the blood was coming from.

"Broken leg," Doyle growled. "My head is bleeding, but I haven't lost consciousness, so I don't think it's bad. My seat belt saved me from going through the window."

"Where's your cell phone?" Dana asked as Nix backed away to call in the accident.

"Somewhere on the floorboard. I tried to get it but…" He waved at his broken leg. "I decided I wasn't about to bleed out and could wait for help to find me. Although I have to admit, I was about to get desperate enough to risk wiggling around again to find the phone."

"Rescue's on the way, Chief." Nix walked back over to the wreck. "What did you hit?"

"The bridge abutment." Doyle waved his right hand backward, groaning as the movement apparently shifted his broken leg.

"Be still, idiot." Dana softened her words with a gentle squeeze of his shoulder.

He looked up at her. "Call Laney, will you?" he asked. "She's probably worried."

"Okay." Dana stepped away and pulled out her cell phone, dialing Laney's number.

Laney answered on the first ring. "Dana?"

"He's been in an accident, but he's alive and making jokes." Out of the corner of her eye, she saw Nix bend in to hear whatever Doyle was saying. Gritting her teeth against the flare of curiosity, she gave Laney a quick rundown of Doyle's injuries. "Rescue's on the way."

"Why couldn't he call?" Laney asked, sounding suspicious, as if she thought Dana wasn't telling her the whole truth.

"His cell phone fell on the floor, and with his broken leg, he couldn't stand the pain of trying to reach it."

"I want to talk to him," Laney said. "Please?"

Dana knew if she'd been in Laney's shoes, she'd have demanded the same thing. She took the phone over to her brother.

Nix backed out, not meeting her gaze, giving

her room to hand over the phone to Doyle. "Laney wants to talk to you," she told him.

As Doyle reassured Laney that he'd live, Dana crossed to Nix, who was shining his flashlight on the road behind the wreck. "What are you looking for?"

He didn't answer, turning the light back toward the truck lying on its side.

"I'm a federal agent," she said quietly. "And I'm Doyle's sister."

"You're on vacation, and he's my boss."

"What did he tell you while I was calling Laney?"

"He just went over what he remembers of the accident."

Such a dodge, she thought. "Which was what?"

Nix's dark eyes turned toward her, gleaming darkly in the reflection of the flashlight beam off the cracked windshield. "He hit the bridge abutment."

"I heard that much." She took the flashlight from his hand and aimed the beam toward the bridge visible about thirty yards behind the wreck. It was a truss bridge, not particularly long, but the land fell away precipitously beyond the nearest edge, and a quick hike down the road re-vealed why. The bridge stood over a deep gorge, at least a thirty-foot drop, with a narrow ribbon of water reflecting starlight below.

If Doyle had missed the abutment and gone over the edge into the gorge…

She shuddered and walked back toward the truck, stopping midway as a sudden thought occurred to her.

"Detective Nix, what's the name of this bridge?" She turned the flashlight toward him, centering the beam on his face so she could read his expression.

He squinted, angling his face away from the light. "Purgatory Bridge."

Dana's heart dipped. She turned slowly and ran the flashlight beam over the delicate ironwork of the bridge, blinking back a sudden burn of tears. She'd crossed this bridge earlier on her way into town. Passed over it without a thought.

Never realizing she'd crossed over the place of her parents' deaths.

She made her way slowly back to the wreck, schooling her features until she was certain her emotions didn't show. She gave the flashlight back to Nix and bent to look in on her brother. He'd finished his conversation with Laney and sat with his hands folded over his chest, clutching her cell phone in his bloodstained fingers.

"You doing okay?" she asked softly.

He looked up, handing over the phone. "Laney wanted to come down here, but I told her to stay put until I find out where the EMTs want to ship me."

Dana glanced at Nix and found him watching them, his expression unreadable. With a sigh, she bent closer to her brother. "What really happened, Doyle? You're a good driver. You didn't just run into a bridge."

He met her gaze, a hint of apology in his green eyes. "And it's your vacation, too," he murmured.

"What happened?"

Closing his eyes, he laid his head against the headrest. "The brakes failed."

A ripple of dread snaked through her. "How long since you had them replaced?"

He rolled his head and opened his eyes to look at her. "Last week."

Nix's voice rumbled behind her, grim as the grave. "Someone tampered with his brakes."

Chapter Two

"Have there been any overt threats?"

Nix looked up at Dana Massey, wondering if she was ever going to run out of restless energy and stop pacing a hole in the waiting-room floor. He'd taken pity on Laney Hanvey, who looked as if she was close to snapping as it was, and removed Doyle's sister to the other end of the waiting area, where she could walk the floor to her heart's content.

"No overt threats," Nix answered when she stopped in front of him, a belligerent look in her mist-green eyes. "But he's not without enemies."

She sank into a chair across from him, as if she'd run out of gas. Stretching her long legs in front of her, she dipped her chin to her chest and looked at him beneath a fringe of dark eyelashes. "So Merritt Cortland is alive, then."

"Can't be sure of that."

"He has the strongest motive."

Nix nodded. "But not the only motive."

"Who else?"

"We haven't yet figured out who else from the police department Cortland might have had on his payroll. The closer we look, the more feathers we ruffle."

"Whose feathers?"

What did she think she was going to do, go run down every police department employee who ever grumbled about the new chief's campaign of cleaning out all vestiges of corruption? There wouldn't be much of a force left. Even those who'd never thought a minute about taking money from Cortland resented being under constant scrutiny. Nix certainly did.

But he knew it was necessary, so he dealt with it. Others in the department weren't quite as sanguine.

"Everybody gets tired of being a suspect," Nix answered.

"Too bad."

He smiled a little at that. "You must be popular with your fellow marshals."

The withering look she shot his way might have stung a lesser man. But Nix shrugged it off. She was tense and upset. And she was clearly a woman of action, so sitting around waiting for someone else to solve the mystery of the tampered brakes had to be driving her crazy.

Ivy Calhoun had volunteered to go with the

vehicle to the garage, leaving Nix to stay with the chief. Massey had asked him to stick close. Nix suspected he wanted someone there at the hospital to protect Laney and Dana.

Not that Dana needed a knight in shining armor. He'd put his money on her in a fair fight.

"Doyle wanted me to go home for the night." She tried to hide it, but Nix heard a hint of hurt behind the words.

"Not a bad idea. The doctors have already told you he'll live, and they've sedated him for the fracture reduction, so he's probably not going to be able to talk to you again before morning."

She winced a little at the term "fracture reduction," the kind of pain-filled grimace that told him she'd suffered a break or two in her time. Not surprising, considering she chased fugitives for a living. "I just worry he's in danger."

"That's what I'm here for," Nix said.

Her eyes narrowed. "And to keep an eye on Laney while he's unconscious?"

He should have known she'd figure it out. "That's my guess."

She pushed out of her slump. "I haven't said 'thanks.'"

"For what? Putting on the brakes in time to keep from smashing into the wreck?"

"For taking the initiative to go look for him in the first place."

"If I hadn't, someone else would have." He nodded toward her. "You were already thinking about it, weren't you?"

"Just say 'you're welcome.'"

He felt a smile crack his face. "You're welcome."

The smile she shot back at him came complete with shiny white teeth and a set of dimples that took ten years off her age. "I don't suppose you could give me directions back to Bitterwood?"

He pulled out his notebook and sketched a quick map for her. "Where are you staying?"

"I told Doyle I'd stay at his place. It's closer than my hotel."

He wondered if that was a good idea. If someone had gone after Doyle's truck, they might have booby-trapped his house, too.

"I'll be careful," she said, correctly interpreting his expression. She was better at reading him than she had a right to be. He'd often prided himself on being inscrutable.

"Okay." He pointed at the map. "This is Old Purgatory Road. Here's the bridge. Cross the bridge and go about a mile past Smoky Joe's Saloon, then take a right on Laurel Road. The chief's house is at the end of the road. Can't miss it."

She waved the sketch at him. "Nice map. Thanks again."

He almost shrugged off her thanks, but remembering her earlier admonition, he put on his best "plays well with others" face and said, "You're welcome. Again."

Ah, there came the dimples. Worth the price of admission.

She passed a pair of new arrivals on the way out, speaking to them quietly before she left. It took Nix a second to place them—Natalie and J. D. Cooper, the chief's friends from Alabama. The redhead nodded a greeting and sat across from Nix in the seat Dana had just vacated. Her husband settled in the chair beside her.

"Detective Nix, right?" Natalie asked by way of a greeting.

Nix nodded.

"Have you seen Doyle since he arrived here?"

"Just briefly when he came in."

"Any idea what caused the accident?"

Nix wasn't sure he was authorized to comment on what was now an ongoing investigation.

Apparently his poker face needed more work than he realized, for Natalie's brow furrowed. "It wasn't an accident, was it?"

Nix cleared his throat. "I can't really comment."

Natalie and her husband exchanged looks. "We'll just ask Doyle and he'll tell us."

"That may be," Nix agreed. "But that's between the chief and you."

Natalie's eyes flashed with irritation, but her husband put a hand on her arm. His touch seemed to settle her. "Fair enough," she said finally. "How did he look when you saw him?"

"Kind of a bloody mess," Nix admitted. "Had a gash on the side of his head that needed stitches, but Doyle said he hadn't lost consciousness, so it looks like the worst of his injuries will be a broken leg." The chief's condition was really more than Nix should have shared with the Coopers, but given his reticence on the nature of the accident, he decided it wouldn't hurt to share a little news that they could get with a phone call to Dana Massey. She hadn't told them about the brake tampering on her way out, however, so he'd keep that information to himself.

"He's a good guy. A good cop," Natalie said, her tone a little defensive.

"Yes, ma'am," Nix agreed.

Her eyes narrowed at his polite tone, but if she thought he was patronizing her, she didn't say so. He wasn't, really. The chief *was* a good guy and, despite his jovial, laid-back management style, he'd already proved himself to be a good cop.

Whether being a good guy and a good cop would be enough to unravel decades of bad practices, indifference and systematic corruption at the Bitterwood P.D. was a question that had yet to be answered.

DOYLE'S NEW HOME turned out to be a two-story log cabin nestled in a small, wooded hollow at the end of Laurel Road. It looked like one of those fancy tourists' cabins you could find a dime a dozen in the Smokies, with names like Eagle's Nest, Black Bear Lodge and Creekview. A large gravel parking area in front of the house suggested that at one time, at least, the cabin had been used for that very purpose.

A wide wooden porch with rustic log rails spanned the front of the house. After retrieving her suitcase and overnight bag from the trunk of her Chevy, she climbed the three shallow steps to the porch and pulled the keys Doyle had given her from the pocket of her jacket.

Seconds from sliding the key into the lock, she heard a noise from inside the cabin.

She fumbled behind her back for her Glock 17 and remembered, with frustration, that she'd packed it in her overnight bag, not wanting to be armed at her brother's engagement party. Setting the bag down as quietly as she could, she crouched and worked open the side zipper, where she'd put her empty Glock and a pair of loaded magazines. Sliding the magazine into the Glock, she chambered a round and tried the door.

Unlocked.

Suddenly, the door flew open. With her hand still on the knob, she overbalanced and staggered through the opening, slamming face-first into something hard and alive.

Whoever hit her kept moving, shoving backward. Wheeling her arms to regain her balance bought her only enough time to hit the log rail with her shoulders instead of the back of her head, not that it saved her much in the way of pain. The crack of bone against wood sent painful tingles shooting down both arms, and the Glock bounced away from her suddenly nerveless fingers, skittering across the porch. The back of her head scraped against the second rail as she hit her tailbone with a jarring thud.

She scrambled for the dropped weapon, but by the time she closed her hands around the grip, the two dark figures running away across the front yard entered the woods and disappeared almost immediately into the gloom.

Grimacing with pain, she sat up and assessed her condition. She'd have a big bruise across her shoulders in the morning and a lump on the back of her head. Plus, she'd broken a heel on a brand-new pair of shoes. But it could have been much worse.

She could have been dead.

She entered the cabin with care, finding the

light switch next to the door and flicking it on. To her surprise, the living room seemed virtually untouched by the intruders she'd just startled.

The same could not be said for the next room she checked. It was a corner room with big windows looking out on the dark woods. In the daytime, she supposed, the windows would probably let in a lot of light, which was probably why Doyle had chosen this particular space as his home office.

Here the intruders had concentrated their efforts. All of the drawers had been pulled out of the walnut desk against the wall, their contents lying scattered across the hardwood floor. File cabinets stood open, spilling papers and files haphazardly from their metal depths. A framed photograph lay torn in its broken frame, a jigsaw puzzle of glass covering the floor in front of it. On the wall above, there was a combination safe. It remained safely shut, though clearly someone had tried to crack the code.

Dana backed out of the study and checked the rest of the house. The kitchen drawers had all been opened and searched, some of their contents now lying in a jumble on the counter and floor. Likewise, Doyle's bedroom had been tossed, an explosion of clothes covering every available surface, thrown aside to assist a thorough search of the chest of drawers by the bed. A second bedroom had received similar treatment, although the mess there was limited because all the drawers and the closet were empty.

Back in Doyle's bedroom, Dana moved aside a faded Lynyrd Skynyrd T-shirt and sank on the end of the bed, pulling out her phone to dial 911. But before she pressed the first number, she changed her mind and called another number instead.

Natalie Cooper answered on the second ring. "Dana. Hi."

"Hi. Are you still at the hospital?"

"Yeah. The doctor just stopped in to reassure us that Doyle was doing fine. They're letting him wake up a little more from the reduction and then they'll put him in a regular room."

"Good," she said, genuinely relieved. Her little brother was strong and tough, but things could still go wrong during any medical procedure. "By any chance is Walker Nix still there?"

"Tall, dark and silent?" Natalie asked, lowering her voice a little.

"That's the one."

"He's across the room staring stoically out the window," Natalie answered in a wry tone. "Why?"

"I need him to call me as soon as possible. Give him my cell number."

"Is something wrong?"

Dana didn't know how to answer that question without potentially sucking Doyle's old friend and former partner into a procedural mess, so she hedged. "Nothing big. I just need to ask Detective Nix something about an ongoing investigation Doyle's been involved with. Can you give him my message?"

"Sure." Natalie hung up and Dana ended the call from her own end, trying not to be immediately impatient for the callback.

It came before she started chewing her nails. "Natalie Cooper said you wanted me to call you?" Nix's gravelly voice rumbled like distant thunder across the telephone line.

"I know you're there to guard Doyle and Laney," Dana said, already beginning to second-guess her decision to bypass emergency response. "Never mind. I'll figure out something else."

"Wait," Nix said before she could end the call. "Something's wrong."

"Yeah," she admitted, looking at the chaos surrounding her in Doyle's bedroom. "Something's very wrong."

DESPITE THE CHAOTIC condition of the chief's study, it was the bloody mass of hair at the back of Dana Massey's head that drew Nix's immediate attention. "Your head is bleeding."

Dana turned away from the mess and lifted her

hand to the back of her head, looking surprised to find blood on her fingers. "I didn't realize."

She looked a little stunned all the way around, Nix thought. She might be a tough lady, but nobody could walk in on a burglary in progress and not be affected. That she'd had the presence of mind to snap a bunch of photos with her cell phone was notable enough. That she'd done it with a goose egg on the back of her head was damned near amazing.

"Am I dripping blood all over the crime scene?" she asked.

"No, seems to be oozing, mostly. It's in your hair and on your shirt."

"Damn it! This blouse is silk."

"I've called a TBI unit in to process the place." The Tennessee Bureau of Investigation offered crime scene investigation for small departments that didn't have the manpower or need for a full-time evidence-retrieval staff.

She frowned. "At this time of night?"

"It's not their usual procedure on a nonviolent case, but with your brother's crash and the possible connection to Merritt Cortland—"

"Yeah," she said with a nod. "I guess that might light a fire under them."

"Why don't we clear out and go somewhere until they can come in and do their work?"

"The burglars might come back."

"So we'll wait for the TBI on the front porch and I'll see what I can do about that bump on your head."

She gave him a look of frustration that he interpreted as irritation that she hadn't caught the intruders single-handedly when she had the chance. He stifled a smile and led her out to the front porch, settling her on the steps while he went to his car to retrieve a first aid kit. When he came back, she had unzipped her bag and was trading out her pumps for a pair of tennis shoes. She waved one of the pumps at him, displaying a broken heel, before she shoved it into her bag.

She sighed and turned the back of her head toward him to give him better access. "How bad is it?"

"Not too bad, really," he said after he'd used some antiseptic to clean the abraded area on the back of her head. "Did they hit you with something?"

She waved her hand toward the porch railing. "They knocked me back into the railing. I hit my head on the bottom rail on the way down. I thought it was just a little bump."

"It is. It's just a bloody one." He applied some antibiotic ointment to the scrape, trying to ignore the way her lightly floral perfume was making his blood run hot. Her hair was thick but soft, sliding over his fingers with the same sensuous texture as warm silk. Her skin was velvety and fragrant, tempting him to bury his face in the curve of her neck and just breathe.

He'd never been a man prone to indulging his every sexual whim, but this particular dose of desire was taking a toll on his legendary self-control, and she wasn't even showing that much skin or giving him any indication that she found him equally attractive.

He backed away, giving himself room to breathe. "I think the bleeding's stopped now. But that shirt may be beyond hope."

She turned on the porch step to face him. "Thanks."

Something intriguing glittered in her eyes, pale and mysterious in the moonlight trickling through the trees. Nix knew it would be folly to speculate what that intriguing something might be. But he'd never been any good at turning his back on a puzzle. Especially one that smelled like wildflowers.

The TBI van came rumbling down the road and parked behind Dana's dark green Chevy Malibu. Nix recognized one of the evidence techs as a man he'd known during his time in the marine corps. He dug in his memory and came up with PFC Brady Moreland. He and Moreland had been at Stone Bay, Camp Lejeune, at the same time about eight years earlier. He and the private had played pool together a few times at Maggie's Drawers, the rec center at Stone Bay.

"Private Moreland," he said aloud as the younger man approached.

Moreland, to his amusement, came close to snapping to attention before his expression shifted with recognition, and a grin spread over his face. "Sarge!"

They shook hands with pleasure; then Nix got down to business, introducing Dana and letting her explain what she'd walked in on.

"It happened too quickly for me to get much of a look at the intruders," she said with regret. "I think they were wearing gloves, but I can't be sure."

"It's okay," the other evidence technician, who introduced himself as Blalock, assured her. "If there's anything here to find, we'll find it."

Dana watched them enter the house, looking as if she wanted to tag along for the search. Nix distracted her by picking up her suitcase, which still lay on its side on the porch.

"I can get that," Dana said, but Nix waved her off.

"I've got it."

"You seem awfully interested in getting me away from here," she said in a tone that was just short of suspicious. He supposed he couldn't blame her for being wary of someone she'd met only a couple of hours earlier under less-than-pleasant circumstances.

"Mostly, I'm interested in getting us both somewhere a little warmer."

She looked as if she wanted to argue, but head-lights appeared in the dark, moving toward them on the narrow, dead-end road. The unmistakable shape of a Ford Mustang finally came into view. Laney Hanvey, Nix thought as the black Mustang squeezed into the narrow space between the TBI van and Nix's truck.

The lady herself got out of the Mustang and hurried to where he and Dana stood on the porch, her gaze widening as she took in Dana's blood-ied condition. "My God, did they attack you?"

"Not on purpose," Dana assured her, though Nix thought she was probably glossing over the violence of what had happened to her. "I just got bowled over and hit the porch rail."

"I should take you to the hospital, get you checked out."

"No," Dana said quickly. "I'm fine, really. It looks worse than it is."

"How's the chief?" Nix asked.

"Groggy. The doctor wants him to stay a day or two, maybe get some rehab for the leg. You can imagine his delight." Laney made a face, but Nix could tell that she was relieved that her fiancé was feeling well enough to complain. "The break-in just gave me an excuse to make him obey his doctor's orders." She glanced at the front door, which the technicians had finally shut, probably to keep out the cold. "How bad is it?"

"A big mess in some rooms," Dana answered. "Not so bad in the others."

"Was anything missing?"

"I'm not sure." Dana looked apologetic. "You'd probably know better than I would."

"I think I'll stick around, then, see what the technicians come up with. Dana, if you'd like to stay at my place tonight, you're welcome. It's over in Barrowville, but that's actually closer to the hospital."

"I don't want to put you out—"

"I'll be going back to the hospital when I'm through here," Laney said with a shrug. "You're welcome to my guest room. The bed's already made up. You can help yourself to anything you can find in the kitchen."

"My car's blocked in," Dana said.

"I'll drive you," Nix offered.

Dana looked at him. "Okay. Thanks."

Nix carried her suitcase to his truck, setting it in the back.

Dana eyed the open truck bed. "Sure it won't tumble out?"

"That's part of the adventure," he murmured in her ear, sneaking a quick whiff of that floral scent that made his gut tighten with desire. He rounded the front of the truck and looked at her across the roof of the cab. "Will it fall out or won't it?"

Her green eyes glittered with amusement in the moonlight. "Easy for you to say. They're not your clothes."

The truck's heater decided to work when Nix cranked the engine, blowing a blast of cold air into his face. On the passenger side, Dana gasped and reached to close the vents.

"Give it a few minutes and it might blow warm," Nix said, buckling up.

Dana looked at him as she belted herself in. "How badly do you want to go home in the next little while?"

He arched an eyebrow. "What do you have in mind?"

Her lips curved in a slow smile. "How about we go see a groggy man with a broken leg about a break-in?"

Chapter Three

Dana's brother was a big guy, tall and well built, as their father had been, but lying in the hospital bed, with his leg propped up and encased in a thick white cast, he seemed shockingly vulnerable and young. His eyes were closed when she and Nix entered his room, but they fluttered open when she pulled up a chair next to his bed.

He smiled a loopy smile and flailed one arm toward her. "Hey there."

She smiled. "Hey yourself."

"Is it morning?" He turned his head toward the window. The curtains were closed, blocking his view of the world outside.

"No, it's just a little after ten. We had to talk our way in past the nurses."

He rubbed his hand over his eyes as if to clear out the sleep. He peered at Nix, who stood quietly near the end of the bed. He gave a nod. "Nix."

Nix's lips hinted at a smile. "Chief."

Doyle's brow furrowed suddenly as he turned

his groggy gaze back to his sister. "How big a mess did they make at my house?"

"Not too bad," she told him, purposefully glossing over the truth to keep him from worrying. She had stopped downstairs in the women's bathroom to change out of her bloodstained shirt into a fresh blouse, but she hadn't been able to comb all of the blood out of her hair, opting to pull her auburn hair back into a ponytail to hide the worst of it. The tug of the elastic on the grazed skin of her scalp wasn't exactly pleasant, but she'd live.

"Laney's there still?"

"Yes. She's going to stay until the evidence technicians get through with their investigation."

"You got the TBI out at this time of night?"

Nix's lips twitched again. "I might have emphasized the fact that you're the chief of police and that there have been previous attempts on your life."

"What were they looking for?" Dana asked.

Doyle's gaze swung back to her. "Certainly not money."

She smiled. "No, I suppose not."

"I don't keep any case files at home," he added. "Although—"

"Although what?" she prodded when he didn't continue.

Doyle glanced toward Nix, not answering.

"I have a phone call to make," Nix murmured, leaving the room almost as quietly as he'd entered it.

Dana pulled her chair a little closer, laying her hand on her brother's arm. "What didn't you want Detective Nix to hear?"

"It's nothing, really. I don't suppose there was any reason to try to keep it secret from him or anyone. It's just—I've come across some strange information recently, and I'm not sure what to think about it."

"What kind of strange information?"

Doyle's focus tightened, and for the first time since Dana had entered the hospital room, he seemed to be fully awake. "Remember a few months ago when I arrested my chief of detectives for kidnapping a local girl?"

"Not exactly the sort of thing I'd be likely to forget," she said drily.

He smiled weakly. "No, I suppose not. Anyway, during the interrogation, Bolen said something that struck me as odd when he was explaining why they'd kidnapped the girl."

"I thought you said it was all about putting pressure on the girl's father to keep the Bitterwood P.D. alive and kicking."

"It was," Doyle said with a nod. "But I didn't tell you the rest of it."

"There's more?"

"A little more. See, there was a point, right before Laney and I managed to turn the tables on Bolen and his boss, that I realized they had deliberately set out to get me up there on the mountain with the missing girl."

Dana hadn't heard this part of the story before. "I thought you just sort of walked into the whole mess."

"Not exactly. At the beginning, Craig Bolen had only agreed to go along with his boss's plan because he thought they could let the girl go free when it was over. But when it became clear that she might have seen or heard too much, they knew they couldn't let her live. So they needed a scapegoat."

"You don't mean *you* were supposed to be the scapegoat."

Doyle shrugged, grimacing a little, as if the movement pained him. "I was new in town. I had a vested interest in keeping the police department going."

"That's ridiculous. Who's going to buy a story like that?"

"That's what I asked Bolen." Doyle covered her hand where it lay on the edge of his bed. "That's when Bolen said something strange. He told me I was a Cumberland, and everybody in Bitterwood knows the Cumberlands are crooks and swindlers and baby-killers. He said no good ever came from a Cumberland in these parts."

Dana frowned. "Mom's maiden name was Cumberland."

"I know."

"She never talked much about her past." Dana looked thoughtfully at her brother. "But we knew she came from somewhere around here, didn't we? That's why she and Dad were here when they had their accident."

"Yes. So I've been doing a little asking around. And while I don't put a whole lot of stock in much of what Craig Bolen has to say these days, he was right about one thing." Doyle's brow furrowed as his troubled gaze met hers. "People around here seem ready to believe the Cumberlands are capable of just about anything bad."

Nix checked his watch, wondering how much longer Dana Massey intended to stay in the room with her brother. He'd already worked a full day and his night hadn't exactly been uneventful. He could use some sleep.

But if he was honest with himself, his growing impatience had less to do with going home and getting some shut-eye and more about getting another eyeful of Dana Massey's long legs, shapely figure and intelligent green eyes.

She is not the woman for you, he reminded

himself, closing his gritty eyes against the harsh artificial light in the otherwise empty waiting room. *And not just because she's leaving town in a few days.*

He wasn't sure that such a woman existed, for that matter. He'd gone thirty-six years without finding a woman who would put up with his cynicism or his emotional reserve. It had been easier to live with that knowledge when he was full-time military, because war was hell on marriages. He'd seen the corrosive effects of long tours of duty, the stress on families trying to stoke the home fires when any moment could bring devastating news from a world away.

But he'd been a civilian for five years now without finding a good woman and settling down.

What's your excuse now, hotshot?

"Falling asleep on me, Detective?"

He opened his eyes at the sound of Dana's low voice. She stood in front of him, the hint of a smile on her lips. But her amusement didn't make it all the way to her eyes. Her night had been even worse than his, and it showed in the faint pallor beneath her tan and the dark shadows under her eyes. "You ready to go?"

She nodded, and he pushed to his feet, falling into step with her as they headed for the elevator. She was quiet all the way to the car, buckling in without speaking. But there was an edge to her silence, hints of a gathering storm.

It struck halfway back to Bitterwood.

"What do you know about the Cumberlands?"

His back stiffened for a second at the sound of the name, and he shot Dana a quick look. In the blue glow of the dashboard lights, her strong profile seemed carved in cool marble, both beautiful and unapproachable.

He'd like to paint her like that, too, he thought.

"Why do you ask?" he said.

"Do you know anything about my family background?"

He didn't like the direction this conversation was going. "No."

"My mother's maiden name was Tallie Cumberland. Ever heard of her?"

The stiffness in his back returned, flowing all the way to his hands until they white-knuckled the steering wheel. The dread ran through him like ice in his blood, freezing him as if he were still that little boy from Cherokee Cove who believed every tale his mama told him, especially the scary ones.

"Don't even look at a Cumberland," she'd warned him from the time he was old enough to walk around on his own two feet. "They're cursed, and they'll spread their sickness on you."

His father hadn't been superstitious at all, but

even he had spoken of the Cumberlands in hushed tones, dire warnings blazing in his eyes.

"You *have* heard of her," Dana said.

"I've heard of the Cumberlands," he admitted.

"Doyle says that when he mentioned the name, people reacted as if he'd just said a curse word."

"Does he know why?"

"Not specifically. The most anyone would tell him is that the Cumberlands are nothing but trouble."

"Does that sound anything like your mother?" he asked carefully.

"No."

"Then I wouldn't worry about it."

Dana didn't say anything else until they reached the Bitterwood city limits. Even then, she merely said she'd told Doyle she was going to stay at his house. "He didn't like it, but I'm older than he is, so I win."

Nix smiled, thinking of his own younger brother and how often he'd invoked the older-sibling rule when they were growing up. "Are you sure you feel safe there? Someone was able to get into the house pretty easily."

"I'm armed and I'm too wired to sleep," she answered, slanting a look of raw determination his way. "Bring it on."

"I could stick around."

"And protect the poor, defenseless girl?"

"Not what I said."

She sighed. "I'm usually not this prickly. It's been an unsettling night."

"I'm serious about sticking around. And not because I don't think you can take care of yourself. But you said there were two intruders. Couldn't hurt to have an extra set of ears to listen out for danger."

"And it wouldn't hurt to have some extra firepower," she admitted. "But it's a lot to ask."

"You didn't ask. I offered."

"So you did." Her lips curved in a smile that softened her features, making her look far more approachable than she had seemed for most of the drive.

Far more dangerous, too, he reminded himself.

The TBI technicians were still there when they arrived, but they were packing up to leave. Laney was outside with them, talking to Brady Moreland. She squinted at the headlights, smiling when she recognized Nix's truck.

"Good timing," she said. "The van will be out of your way in just a minute."

"Actually, I'm staying here tonight after all," Dana told her as she slid out of the cab of the truck. "I ran by to see Doyle and told him I'd keep an eye on the place."

"Oh." Laney looked surprised. "Okay. I need to run home and get some notes for a court case that starts Monday, but I can be back here in a half hour—"

"You don't have to stay with me," Dana said quickly. "Doyle told me you'd probably try but to remind you your big case is important and I'm a deputy U.S. marshal with a big gun."

"Are you sure?"

"Positive. Go get some rest so you can kick butt in court Monday."

After Laney's taillights disappeared around the bend, Dana turned to look at Nix. "I do appreciate the offer to stay, but—"

"But you're a deputy U.S. marshal with a big gun?"

She patted her purse. "Glock 17."

"Nice." He bent a little closer to her, lowering his voice. "I have a sweet Colt 1911 .45 caliber with a rosewood grip, and if you quit trying to get rid of me, I might let you hold it."

A dangerous look glittered in her eyes. "You're trying to tempt me with an offer to handle your weapon?"

He nearly swallowed his tongue.

She smiled the smile of a woman who knew she'd scored a direct hit. "You can stay," she said almost regally. "We'll negotiate weapon-handling terms later."

She headed up the porch steps and entered

her brother's house, leaving Nix to wonder just what he'd gotten himself into.

DANA GAVE NIX the guest room, taking her brother's bedroom for herself. As she was trying to figure out what part of the chaos to tackle first, Nix knocked on the door frame. He paused in the doorway, eyeing the mess with a grimace. "Let me help you straighten up."

"It's okay. I can get it."

"You should take a shower and clean the blood out of your hair," he said firmly. "Go ahead. I'll see how far I can get by the time you're done."

She was too tired and sore to argue. The bruises on her shoulders were beginning to ache, and the blood in her hair was giving off an unpleasant metallic odor she would be happy to get rid of. She took her whole suitcase into the bathroom down the hall, pleased to see that the room conformed to tourist mountain cabin standards by being roomy and, even better, boasting a whirlpool tub with a multisetting handheld showerhead.

She tried to hurry through her bath, but the soothing pulse of the showerhead's massage setting against her bruised shoulders was seductive, keeping her in the tub longer than she'd intended. She forced herself out of the hot spray finally, gritting her teeth against the faint chill of the bathroom on her wet skin, and hurried through drying off and dressing.

But by the time she reached Doyle's bedroom, Nix had finished most of the cleanup, changing the bedsheets and returning most of the clothes back to their drawers. "There were a few things smudged with fingerprint powder," he told her as he wiped down the dresser surface with a damp rag. "I put those and the sheets in the clothes basket in the laundry room."

"Where's the laundry room?" she asked, tugging her robe more tightly around her as Nix's dark-eyed gaze dropped to where the robe lapels gaped open to reveal her thin nightgown.

His gaze snapped back up to meet hers. "Just off the kitchen."

"Ah."

"Was the water hot enough?"

She nodded. "Bathroom's amazing. What is this place, one of those tourist cabins?"

"Actually, I think it may be," Nix answered, giving the chest of drawers a final swipe of the dust rag. "Back about ten years ago, some guy bought up a lot of this land and built a bunch of cabins, hoping to bring more tourism to this area. But it's just too far off the beaten path, and Bitterwood doesn't have enough attractions to compete with places like Gatlinburg, Pigeon Forge or Bryson City. So the guy had to sell off a bunch of these cabins for a song just to keep his real-estate business from going belly-up. Doyle probably got a decent deal on the place. Is he buying or renting, do you know?"

"Buying," she answered. "He said it wouldn't look good for the chief of police to rent a place. Might make it seem like he wasn't planning to stick around for the long haul. Bad optics."

Nix's grimace suggested he wasn't a fan of that sort of public-service politics. Dana didn't like it much herself, though being a federal law enforcement agent meant that some level of politics was unavoidable.

"Thanks for cleaning up," she added, waving her hand toward the much neater room.

"Not a problem."

As Nix took a step toward the bedroom door, Dana caught his arm, stilling his movement. He looked down at her hand, then slowly lifted his gaze back to her face. Heat radiated from his tall, broad-shouldered body, washing over her in a flood that set her own skin tingling.

"Yes?" His voice was like silk over sandpaper.

"You know something about my mother, don't you?"

Nix recoiled slightly, the movement clearly involuntary. Dana stared at him, watched the color suffuse his face as his gaze slid.

Her pulse notched upward, fueled by a river of

dread flowing through her veins to settle in the center of her chest. She took her own step backward, until her knees hit the edge of Doyle's bed and she sat abruptly, curling her fingers into the bedspread.

"What did my mother do?" she asked, her voice tight with alarm.

Nix made himself look at her, his dark gaze unfathomable. "If the story I've heard all my life is true, she killed her own baby and tried to steal someone else's."

Chapter Four

Dana's face went pale with shock at Nix's words. She stared at him, first in stunned silence, then in a slowly simmering anger that chased the pallor from her face, replacing it with splotches of high color in her cheeks.

"That's ludicrous."

He didn't know what to say. He couldn't actually vouch for any of the details. All he knew was what the older people in his small community had whispered for years, quietly enough that they could pretend discretion while knowing full well that their children were listening and absorbing the cautionary tale of the teenage girl who got herself pregnant, got away with murder and eventually got herself run out of town for her sins.

"My mother was a wonderful, kind, smart and decent woman."

"I'm sure she was," Nix agreed, though not with enough conviction to drive the fury from Dana's flashing eyes.

"You couldn't possibly know anything about her. She left here before you were born."

"Yeah, about a year before I was born," he agreed.

She looked away from him, as if she couldn't stand looking at him any longer. He took that as his cue to leave, backing toward the door.

"Wait," she snapped.

He faltered to a stop.

She looked at him again, her expression more composed, though distress roiled behind her eyes. "Please sit." She waved her hand toward the armchair by the window, next to a table holding a reading lamp and a small stack of books.

He sat in the chief's chair and took a bracing breath before he looked at Dana again, steeling himself against her anger and pain. But she seemed to have herself completely under control now, her expression back to cool neutral, her eyes mirrors reflecting her surroundings without revealing anything that lay beneath.

"Where did you hear that story about my mother?" she asked.

She wasn't going to let it go, he saw. Not that he should have expected her to. After all, she hadn't chosen a career in law enforcement because she was incurious or prone to dodging conflict.

"It's one of those stories you grow up hearing," he answered carefully.

"Like monsters in the closet and bogeymen under the bed?" she asked, only a hint of sarcasm breaking the calm surface of her composure.

"Yes," he admitted. "Like that."

"So, tell me. What was the story? How did she kill her child?"

"Her baby," he corrected. He thought he saw a quick flinch, a slight tightening in the corners of her eyes. "She was unmarried. Pregnant. Went into labor and someone took her to the hospital in Maryville for delivery. Everything went okay and the baby was born." He faltered to a stop, knowing the worst part of the story, the part that made any normal person recoil, was yet to come.

"Did she kill the baby at the hospital or at home?" Dana asked, her tone businesslike, as if she were interviewing a witness to a crime.

"At the hospital. The nurse had brought him for feeding and left him there with her. As the story goes, she claims she fell asleep and someone switched out her live baby for an already dead one. But nobody saw anything."

"Nobody saw anyone carrying a dead baby into the room or carrying a live one out, you mean."

"Right." Nix shook his head. "Dana, I don't know that any of this is true. It's just a story."

"Maybe." She shrugged. "Maybe not. What happened when the unmarried girl discovered the baby in the bassinet was dead?"

"She started screaming." He swallowed a lump that had formed in his throat as he watched Dana's face grow even stonier. "She kept screaming at the nurses that it wasn't her baby, but of course, it had to be. Nobody had gone into her room."

"That anyone witnessed."

He'd let his gaze drift away from her face but snapped it back at her words. "That anyone witnessed."

"What's the next part of this cautionary tale?" Her voice held a minute trace of sarcasm, so tiny he wasn't sure whether it was really there or he was just reading that tone into her words.

"The hospital called in a psychiatrist to calm her down. She finally settled down and started to cooperate with the hospital staff, who were trying to make arrangements for the baby's burial. The nurse who saw her just before all hell broke loose supposedly swore she seemed to be sad but acting normally enough for a girl who'd just lost her newborn baby."

Dana was silent and very still for a long moment. When she spoke, her voice was faint and strained. "And then?"

"The nurses supposedly heard screams coming from a room down the hall on the same floor. A woman screaming that someone had stolen her baby. The story goes, they locked down the hospital and finally found the unmarried girl and the missing baby in the hospital basement. She was trying to take him out a service exit."

"Who were the baby's parents?"

"You mean the baby that lived?"

She nodded.

"I don't know," he admitted. "That was never part of the story I heard."

"They only identified the girl?"

He nodded. "Crazy Tallie Cumberland, mad as a hare and wicked as the rest of her family. Killed her own baby and tried to steal another. Better take care and not let a Cumberland look you in the eye, or you'll turn out crazy and wicked, too."

"Lovely."

"I'm sorry. I guess it's not so entertaining a legend when you're on the Cumberland end of things."

"It's also completely impossible," Dana said in a low, flat tone. "My mother couldn't have killed her own child under any circumstances. She was perfectly sane, perfectly rational and as loving and protective a mother as a child could have hoped for."

"I'm sure you're right," Nix said.

"No, you're not." She pulled the collar of her robe more tightly around herself. "You never knew her."

"No, I didn't." Nix stood. "It's late. We're tired.

Let's just get some sleep tonight while we can. Morning will make everything look better."

At least, he hoped it would.

But long after he retreated to the guest room, he remained awake, staring at the moon-painted ceiling over the bed and wondering just how much of the story he'd told Dana was true.

And how much of it, true or otherwise, had led to Doyle Massey's brand-new brakes failing on the curve just past Purgatory Bridge?

LOSING HER PARENTS had been one of the most devastating moments of Dana Massey's life. She'd talked to her mother on the phone only a couple of hours before the accident, planning for a birthday party for David, the baby of the family, which was to have taken place the next month. David was turning eighteen, a significant milestone, and Tallie Massey had tasked Dana with finding a particular set of books David wanted for his birthday. They were obscure books on South American agricultural technology, in the original Spanish, and neither of her parents had a clue where to start looking.

Dana had been a junior in college, entirely too full of herself and far too certain she knew everything there was to know about any subject of importance.

Stupid, stupid girl.

The call had come in the middle of the night. It had been David, the baby, the one who felt everything like a pierce to the heart, trying so hard to be strong and adult, to break the news to her gently.

But there was no easy way to tell someone her parents were dead.

Doyle had beaten her home by an hour. She'd found him and David sitting in silence in the well-worn den of their family home, staring at the phone as if waiting for more bad news to crash down on them. They'd looked up in unison as she entered the room, just staring at her with shattered expressions and heartsick eyes. She'd opened her arms and David had run to her, a lost little boy in a young man's body.

"Sheriff Morgan delivered the news himself," Doyle had told Dana later, after they'd coaxed David into getting some sleep before morning came and the food-and-sympathy visits started. "David said he'd offered to stick around, but our little brother didn't want us to think he was still a kid."

Oh, David, Dana thought, staring at the ceiling of her brother's bedroom. *What kind of man would you have been?*

Morning light was beginning to seep through the curtains, just a hint of pearly-gray in the otherwise unrelenting darkness, but it gave her an excuse to get out of bed and get her mind out of the bleak past for a while.

There was a light on in the kitchen, the sound of water running. Figuring an intruder wouldn't stop for a drink of water, she decided against going back into the bedroom for her Glock and entered the kitchen to find Walker Nix scooping coffee grounds into a filter. He turned at the sound of her bare footsteps on the hardwood floor. "Did I wake you?"

"No." She stifled a yawn and settled on one of the stools in front of the breakfast bar. "You're up early."

"I have to go home and get ready for work."

"Right."

He looked at her over his shoulder, his dark eyes hooded. "You want some coffee?"

She nodded. "Nice and strong, I hope?"

"Of course." His lips twitched as he reached into the cabinet over the coffeemaker and pulled out a couple of large mugs. "Did you get any sleep?"

She grimaced. "That obvious, huh?"

"You look fine." He actually sounded as if he believed what he was saying.

"You're a better diplomat than you look," she murmured with a smile.

He left the coffee percolating and pulled up the stool beside hers, resting one arm on the bar and turning to face her. "I want you to forget what I told you last night about your mother. I have no proof that any of it happened, and what passes as truth, in these hills, can be as flexible as taffy."

"I know it didn't happen the way you heard it," she said with confidence. "But something happened to my mother when she was living here in Bitterwood. There's no other reason why she would've hidden her past so thoroughly from us for all these years."

"You didn't even know she was from here?"

"I knew she was from the Smoky Mountains. That she was born in Tennessee and didn't meet my father until she was nearly twenty and working at a bait shop in Terrebonne. She told us she didn't have any family left, and no reason to go back to Tennessee for visits. That's why we were sort of surprised when she and my dad decided to drive to Tennessee for their vacation."

"Do you think your father knew about your mother's past?"

She thought about the question for a moment. "I think so. They were best friends as well as spouses. They didn't keep secrets from each other."

"But they never told you or your brother anything about it?"

"No." She hadn't thought much about why her mother's past was a blank. It had simply always been that way, for as long as she remembered. "I think Dad guarded her secret because that's what she wanted. But he must have known."

"She didn't leave you anything, a written journal or something that might have explained the blanks in her past?"

"No. Nothing. She wasn't expecting to die, so she hadn't prepared."

"My mother got real sick when I was sixteen," Nix said after a moment of silence. "Breast cancer. She just wanted to live at least long enough to get me and my brother out of high school." Nix's smile was tinged with a hint of exasperation. "Lavelle had to be pushed through that final semester, kicking and screaming."

"Younger brothers," Dana murmured, biting back the urge to cry.

"The good news is, she beat the cancer. Twenty-year survivor as of January."

She felt a flutter of relief. "That's wonderful."

He nodded. "The chief says you're the oldest."

"He likes to remind people of that a lot. Lucky me."

"If it makes you feel any better, you look younger."

"Ten years ago, I might have smacked you for saying that," she said with a grin. "But now I'll just say 'thanks.' And suggest you might want to get your eyes checked."

He looked at her for a long moment, his scrutiny straightforward and a little unnerving. "You have to know you're a very attractive woman."

She supposed she knew it, although the deeper into her thirties she went, the more she had a sense of time ticking past her at a quicker rate. She'd put her career first, her personal life a distant second, and she'd been okay with that order of things, because she'd always figured there'd be time, before her youth was spent, to change her priorities.

But she was two months shy of her thirty-fifth birthday, no longer the youngest, prettiest woman in any given room, and her expectations had changed.

"Thank you, again." She cocked her head, smiling slightly. "You're brave, Detective Nix. Flirting with the chief's sister."

"Oh, sugar, this ain't flirting," he said in a drawl so low and sexy her cheeks started burning.

"Just as well," she murmured, retreating to the counter, where the coffee had finished burbling. She poured the hot black liquid into a mug and crossed to the refrigerator for milk. She spotted some hazelnut liquid creamer—had to be there for Laney, she figured, since Doyle didn't care for sweet coffee—and poured a dollop from the container into her cup.

"You're involved with someone back in Atlanta?" Nix asked. He'd moved to the counter to pour his own cup of coffee. Like Doyle, he drank it black, no cream, no sugar.

"Not at the moment."

He glanced up from his coffee cup, a flame flickering in his dark eyes. She felt a responding flood of heat deep in her abdomen and forced her gaze back to her own coffee.

"Not in the market?"

"I don't consider myself a commodity," she answered a little more tartly than she'd intended.

Nix's eyebrows twitched slightly, but he didn't seem particularly offended by her response. "I'll take that as a no."

Still, she felt bad about snapping at him just for showing mild interest in her availability. She should feel flattered. Hell, she *was* flattered; Walker Nix was an attractive man. It wasn't his fault that she didn't care to involve herself in a short-term, dead-end fling.

She pushed her hair back from her face, meeting his gaze. "Sorry. I've spent a long time trying to get my fellow marshals to treat me like one of the guys. I forget my social graces sometimes."

"I'd rather you just say what you're thinking, straight out. Honesty goes a long way."

"Okay. Then, honestly, I'm here in Bitterwood for two weeks. I'm not sticking around after that."

"And you're not interested in a short-term fling?" The corner of his mouth twitched as he cut to the chase.

"Not that you were offering?"

"No," he said, the twitch becoming a whisper of a smile. "I wasn't offering. For pretty much the same reason."

She let out a long, slow breath. "Well, then."

He walked slowly across the narrow space between them, reaching past her to put his mug of coffee on the breakfast bar. The move brought him so close she felt his heat pour over her, igniting another blaze of heat in her center. He bent his head, his breath hot against her ear. "Not that it ain't mighty damn tempting."

He stepped back, flashed her a smile that she felt right down to the tips of her toes and headed out of the kitchen toward the front door.

"You're leaving already?" she asked, her voice embarrassingly hoarse.

He turned in the open doorway. "You may be on vacation, Marshal. But I'm not." He lifted his hand in a brief, stationary wave, then pulled the door shut behind him.

She forced herself to stay where she was rather than trail him to the door and watch him leave. She might be feeling like a giddy school-girl right down to her tingling toes, but she had her pride.

And more important, she reminded herself sternly, she had a mystery to unravel. She just had to figure out where to start.

As she was walking back to the bedroom, the house phone started ringing. She picked up the bedroom extension, bracing herself to explain to the caller that her brother wasn't available.

But it was Nix. "Sorry—I meant to mention this before I left. I don't know how much truth there is to that story about your mother, but there's a way you can find out."

"Yeah?"

"In the story I've always heard, your mother was penniless, a charity case. And the couple whose baby boy she tried to take were well-off and reputable, which made what she did that much more scandalous."

"If it really happened."

"If it happened," he conceded. "But if even a germ of the story is true, then what you're look-ing for is a hospital that would treat both indigent and wealthy patients."

"In other words, not a charity hospital or a low-income care facility."

"Right. And there's really only one hospital

close that fits that description. Maryville Mercy Hospital."

"That's the hospital where Doyle is."

"That's right. Good luck." He hung up the phone.

Good luck, she repeated silently. She had a feeling she was going to need all the luck she could find to cut through the years of rumor and innuendo to get to the truth about her mother's secret life in Bitterwood.

But Maryville Mercy Hospital was as good a place to start as any.

Chapter Five

Nix walked slowly across the narrow two-lane street that bisected tiny Purgatory, Tennessee, wondering how long Alexander Quinn planned to keep him waiting. He hadn't even taken his seat in the detectives' office at the police station when his phone rang, and a low voice informed him that Merritt Cortland had been spotted in Purgatory.

It had been a few years since Nix had spoken to the old spymaster, but even with the man's voice disguised, there was a certain tone to it that Nix found unforgettable. Many things had changed since the last time they'd met—Nix now carried a badge, not an M-16, and Quinn had recently left the CIA to start his own investigative agency in Purgatory. But Nix had a feeling Quinn would never fully give up his secret-agent ways.

Case in point—luring Nix to Purgatory with an anonymous tip. Nix doubted anyone had spotted Merritt Cortland anywhere near Purgatory.

Which meant Quinn wanted him to come to Purgatory for some other reason but didn't want to approach him directly.

On the other side of the road, Laurel Park was little more than a scenic overlook, a narrow strip of grass and trees that ended about thirty yards off the road where Little Black Creek meandered through the foothills just west of the Smokies. In the late nineteenth century, Purgatory had been a company town for a nearby Tennessee marble quarry, but by the end of the Second World War, the company had gone bankrupt as the demand for less expensive building materials drove most of the state's marble quarries out of business.

Fortunately, the Great Smoky Mountains National Park was in business by then, and Purgatory, like other towns near the park's border, had made a trade out of tourism for a couple of decades before other towns closer to the park and more easily accessible by interstate highway had lured most of the tourists away.

Now Purgatory was limping along on the back of a large auto parts plant that had opened in Barrowville. Corporate bigwigs at the plant had looked east to Purgatory for land on which to build large homes and estates that would provide them with both an easy commute and the pristine beauty of living in the mountains.

The town's name was unfortunate, but some

folks around Ridge County would argue that it was well-enough earned, since the little town had struggled more than thrived for most of its existence.

Nix settled on a wooden bench to wait for Quinn to make himself known. That he was watching from some hiding place was a given. Nix couldn't imagine Quinn waiting in the open for someone to approach him first.

A man with long sandy-brown hair strolled slowly toward him. His knee-length hiking shorts, round, red-lensed sunglasses, grimy baseball cap and well-worn backpack were the typical uniform of a section hiker, one of hundreds of thousands who hiked the Appalachian Trail section by section over the course of several years.

Of course, even if Nix hadn't recognized the long-haired man as the former CIA agent he'd come to see, he'd have been suspicious, since the Appalachian Trail was several miles to the east of Purgatory, winding along the Tennessee/North Carolina state line.

The hiker otherwise known as Alexander Quinn sat at the other end of the bench from Nix and pulled a water bottle from his backpack. "Warm weather's finally here," he said with just enough of a hipster vibe to make Nix bite back a laugh.

"That's a new look for you," Nix murmured.

"Recycled from about twenty years ago," Quinn said in his normal accent, a neutral tone that had a chameleon-like ability to sound as if it could originally have come from almost any English-speaking country. "Thanks for coming."

"Was there really a Merritt Cortland sighting?"

"Actually, there was, although I can't vouch for it personally," Quinn answered. His gaze moved lazily from side to side, as if he were just a tourist enjoying the view. But Nix knew the old spymaster never did anything casually.

"Are you expecting company?"

"Expecting? No." He took another swig from his water bottle, then slipped it into the backpack that sat on the bench between them. "But it never hurts to stay alert."

"Are you planning to get to the point of my summons?"

Quinn's eyes met his briefly. "My agency has been looking into Cortland's disappearance. That's how we got the tip that someone may have seen him just north of here, near the old marble quarry."

"How valid a tip?"

"Remains to be seen. But we haven't come across any proof that Cortland is dead, either. So we have to proceed on the assumption that he could still be alive and kicking. And if so, he's probably working overtime to solidify his control of his father's criminal enterprise."

"Why are you telling me this?" Nix asked.

"Seemed like something you'd want to know."

"It's something a lot of people would like to know. The FBI, the U.S. Marshals Service—"

"I hear someone tried to kill your chief of police." Quinn leaned back, crossing his ankle on top of his knee. The soles of his hiking boots were muddy and well-worn, Nix noticed. When the man donned a disguise, he didn't miss a beat.

"That's still under investigation," Nix said carefully.

Quinn laid his head back, as if enjoying the morning sun that angled through the trees overhead to bathe his face with warm light. "Check with your office. I believe you'll find the mechanic's assessment is in."

Nix stared at Quinn. "I thought you were out of the spy business."

He shrugged. "I don't spy for the *government* anymore."

"Just for yourself?"

"Let's just say I haven't lost the ability to uncover sensitive information when necessary."

"Do the people you employ know you're still playing head games?"

"They know me," Quinn said simply.

Nix supposed that response answered the question about as well as anything would. "So, you've told me there may or may not have been a Cortland sighting in the area. A phone call would have sufficed."

"Well, there's also this." Quinn reached into his pocket and pulled out a smartphone. Punching a couple of buttons, he brought up a photograph of a man in his early thirties with a shaggy beard the color of dark rust, wavy dark hair that fell to his broad shoulders and a lupine smile that didn't quite reach his crystal blue eyes. The first thought that came to Nix's mind was "charisma"—the bearded man seemed to have it, even in the flat, lifeless cell phone photo. His second thought was that the man looked very familiar.

"Who is he?"

"He seems to be the face of the Blue Ridge Infantry these days." Quinn shut off the phone and slipped it back into his pocket. "His name is Blake Culpepper."

Culpepper. Nix tried not to react, but Quinn hadn't been a successful spy for decades without honing his observational skills to a razor's edge.

"I believe you might know some Culpeppers," he said lightly.

"A few," Nix admitted. The Culpeppers of Cherokee Cove were nearly as notorious as the Cumberlands, though their crimes had never included infanticide or baby stealing. Just theft, drunk and disorderly and any number of assaults and batteries arising out of too much liquor and too many women suckered in by Culpepper men genetically blessed with good looks, passable brains and a seemingly endless supply of hill-billy charm.

Blake Culpepper had been a contemporary of his brother, Lavelle, prone to sucking Nix's younger sibling into all sorts of trouble during their teenage years. He'd been clean-shaven back in those days. More baby-faced. But all the signs of danger had been there.

"So he's the new boss, then?" he asked.

"Or he's acting as Cortland's first lieutenant," Quinn answered with a shrug. "We're not sure which."

"And that's why you called me here," Nix guessed. "You want me to find out what Blake Culpepper's up to."

"It's the first time a Tennessee member of the crew has reached this level of prominence," Quinn said quietly. "The Virginia contingent was firmly in charge before now. We're of the opinion that Blake's sudden prominence may be more about what's going on at the head of the whole criminal enterprise, not just limited to control of the militia group."

"I'm not exactly privy to the goings-on of the

Blue Ridge Infantry, even if I am from Cherokee Cove."

"You're more privy than any of us," Quinn answered, smiling as he repeated Nix's old-fashioned word choice.

Nix sighed. "So, what are my marching orders, sir?"

"I'm not your boss. I'm just giving you information you can choose to use as you see fit." Quinn stood up, made a show of stretching his muscles as if preparing for another long hike. "Consider it my contribution to civil society." He wandered off much as he'd come, unhurriedly and without even a hint of self-consciousness.

Nix remained on the bench a few moments longer, gazing at the burbling creek as he thought about what few nuggets of information Quinn had bothered to share. Clearly the old spymaster thought Blake Culpepper was an important link in the chain of petty criminals who had formed Wayne Cortland's original band of knaves. Maybe the most important link, if it turned out that Merritt Cortland hadn't survived his fall from Copperhead Ridge.

But how was Nix supposed to exploit his Cherokee Cove connection? Everybody around Bitterwood knew he was a cop. Especially the folks from his little hometown community. It wasn't as though he could worm his way into the Culpepper inner circle.

Unless…

He pulled out his phone and dialed a number. After several rings, a machine picked up and a low, musical voice with a considerable mountain drawl informed him to leave a message.

He hung up instead, preferring to speak in person to the one person named Culpepper who might just give him the time of day.

"WITHOUT A WARRANT, I can't release any information to you," the hospital administrator told Dana with a halfhearted look of apology. "If you can arrange a warrant, or get permission from the people involved—"

"The woman whose baby died was my mother," Dana said, trying not to let her frustration show. She knew the rules as well as Dr. Sandlin and was grateful that the administrator had taken a moment out of her busy day to hear what Dana had to say. "She died fifteen years ago in Bitterwood. I just need to know if the story is true."

"I wish I could help you," Dr. Sandlin said. "I truly do. But my hands are tied. You're talking about something that happened almost forty years ago. Even if I could look up the records, which I'm not sure I could at this point, warrant or no warrant, the facts would probably be pretty dry and uninformative. Have you tried speaking to your mother's family?"

"I haven't been able to track down any of them," she answered truthfully.

"Well, if I were you, that's where I'd start looking for information." Dr. Sandlin stood, her posture dismissive.

Tamping down her irritation at walking into another brick wall, Dana left the administrator's office and headed down the corridor to the elevator alcove. At least the trip to the hospital wasn't a complete bust. She could stop in to see her brother for a while, maybe help him coax his doctor into letting him go home.

But Doyle wasn't in his room when she got there. She flagged down a nurse passing outside his room. "I'm looking for Doyle Massey."

"I believe he's down in physical therapy," the nurse answered.

"Thank you." Dana started to turn back to the room, then stopped. "Excuse me, Nurse?"

The nurse turned back to look at her, smiling but unable to hide a hint of impatience. "Yes?"

"Do you know of any nurses who would have worked at this hospital maybe thirty-five or forty years ago? In the maternity ward."

The nurse frowned, as if she found the question strange. Dana supposed it was a pretty odd request, but it didn't hurt to ask.

"I don't know if she worked the maternity ward back then, but Doris Kingsley has worked here at Mercy her whole career. She only works part-time these days, though. I'm not sure if she's on duty today."

"What floor does she work on?"

"Seventh." The nurse smiled suddenly. "That's the nursery."

"Thank you." Dana went back into Doyle's room to retrieve her purse and headed for the seventh floor.

It didn't take long to pick out a likely suspect. Plump and motherly-looking, with short gray hair that fell in curls around her smiling face, the nurse was wheeling a newborn down the hall to one of the maternity rooms when Dana stepped out of the elevator and almost directly into her path.

Dana pulled up quickly before she collided with the bassinet. "Oops!"

The nurse smiled at her. "No harm."

Before she made it all the way past, Dana took a stab. "Are you Doris?"

The nurse pulled up and looked more closely at her. Her brow furrowed, and a look of puzzlement came over her round face. "Do I know you?"

"No, but if you're Doris Kingsley, it's possible you knew my mother. Tallie Cumberland."

Doris's expression changed immediately, but

not to scorn or dismay. Instead, her eyes seemed to light up with pleasure. "Bless her heart. So she had herself another baby, then."

"Three of us," Dana answered with a smile of her own, then looked down at the wriggling baby. Blue cap, blue booties. Must be a boy. "I know you need to get this little fellow to his mother, but when you have a spare moment, could we talk? I need to ask you a few questions about my mother."

"I go on a break as soon as I deliver little Jordan here to his mama. There's a break room just down the hall, right before you get to the waiting area. Go on in there, and if anyone asks why you're there, you tell 'em you're waiting for me."

Dana did as she asked, settling at the small break-room table. Nobody else entered until Doris showed up about five minutes later.

"I've wondered about your mama for over thirty years," Doris said without preamble, pouring herself a cup of coffee from the carafe warming on a nearby burner. "She was so sad, so troubled after her baby died. I really worried she wasn't ever going to be able to get over it. How's she doing?"

"I'm afraid my mother died in a car accident fifteen years ago."

Doris sank into the chair across from Dana, her expression falling. "Oh. I'm so sorry to hear that."

"She had a lot of happiness before that. Three kids who loved her like crazy and a husband who thought she hung the moon," Dana assured her, blinking back tears of her own. "But she never told us about her experience here all those years ago, and I need to know all I can about what happened to her."

Doris reached across the table and patted Dana's hand. "Honey, I don't know that digging up old bones that way is going to make you feel any better."

Dana knew the woman was probably right. But she needed to know about her mother's past for more reasons than just assuaging her own curiosity and sense of unease about what she'd learned. It was possible, though perhaps not likely, that Doyle's attempts to find out what had happened to their mother all those years ago had put him in danger. If the story Nix had told her was true, their mother had tried to take a baby that she believed had been stolen from her. That baby was probably still alive. His parents were probably still alive.

And if her mother's version of the story, however wild it might seem, was true, the other couple would have a pretty good reason to want Doyle and his sister to disappear and stop dredging up history.

Reason enough to make sure the nosy chief of police met with an unfortunate accident?

"I understand if you don't want to talk about it," she said to Doris. "But I need a place to start looking."

"I didn't say I wouldn't talk about it," Doris said. "I just wanted to be sure you're ready to hear what happened."

Dana's stomach turned a flip at the serious look in the nurse's eyes. But she stiffened her spine. "I'm ready."

"What have you been told about your mother's experiences here at the hospital?" Doris asked.

As briefly as she could, Dana told Doris the story that Nix had imparted to her, leaving out nothing, no matter how insulting to her mother. As she spoke, she saw Doris's expression grow first troubled, then indignant.

"Oh, honey, if that's what you've heard, no wonder you want answers," Doris said when Dana fell silent. "It's a bunch of half-truths and flat-out lies. I can promise you that."

Even though she'd known in her heart that Nix's story was a gross mischaracterization, Dana felt a little thrill of relief to hear Doris Kingsley's reassurance. "So what's true and what's not?"

"It's true your mama came here to the hospital to have her baby. A little boy. And it's true she wasn't married. She didn't talk about the father or anything like that. She was focused only on that sweet little baby." Doris's gentle eyes grew sad. "She loved that baby boy."

"Did she pick a name for him?"

"She didn't get a chance."

Dana took a deep breath. "What happened to the baby?"

"The doctors said sudden infant death syndrome. Back then, we knew less about how to prevent it. And he was in two of the high-risk categories—born to a teenage mother from a poverty situation."

"So there was never any question that my mother did something to her baby?"

Doris gave her a pained look. "I'm sorry to say, there was an investigation. But the doctor had seen SIDS cases before, and that poor little baby had all the signs. Your mama didn't do a thing to that baby but love him."

Dana blinked, spilling tears that had formed in her eyes. She dashed them away with her fingertips. "What about later? Did she try to take someone else's baby?"

"I think losing her son put your mama in a very bad place." Doris's voice was gentle but firm. "Anything she did was out of that pain."

"So she did try to take another couple's baby."

"I can't tell you the name of the couple. I know who they were, but we have privacy laws—"

"I'm a deputy U.S. marshal. I understand about laws," Dana said quickly, afraid Doris would stop before she told everything that had happened. "Just the basics will do."

"Your mama became convinced her baby had been switched with the dead baby. Coincidentally, the only other couple in the maternity ward at the time of her baby's death came from the same town as your mother."

So the other couple had been from Bitterwood, too. That could help her narrow the possibilities. "What made my mother think there was a switch?"

"She said the dead baby didn't look like her son." Doris shook her head. "I wasn't on duty when it happened. I never saw the baby's body, but I know that people don't look the same when they're dead as when they're alive. And with babies, who can look so much alike anyway—"

"She was seeing what she wanted to see," Dana finished for her.

"I think she must have been, don't you?"

Dana supposed it was the most likely answer. Grief could make the whole world look like an alien landscape, even a world as familiar to you as the sound of your own voice. She'd experienced deep, crushing grief twice in her life so far. The world had changed drastically for her both times.

What must it have been like for her mother,

alone, scared and clinging to the one good thing in her life, only to see it taken from her so quickly and cruelly?

"She dressed up like a nurse's aide and took the other family's baby in his bassinet as if she was taking him back to the nursery. They discovered what she'd done just a couple of minutes later when the real nurse's aide came for the child," Doris continued. "The hospital went on lockdown. They caught her trying to take the baby out through the employees' exit on the ground floor."

"Was she arrested?"

"Yes, but the other family didn't want to press charges, once they had their baby back and learned about her own loss. The police made her go see a psychiatrist instead of putting her in jail. That's the last I heard about her, one way or another. But I've often wondered what happened to her."

Impulsively, Dana pulled out her billfold and showed Doris the last picture her family had taken together. It was an impromptu shot, taken by a friend of her father's during a camping trip near Terrebonne Bay. They were all there—her parents, she and Doyle looking as bored and embarrassed as the college students they'd been at the time, and young David, mugging for the camera and flashing devil's horns behind Doyle's head.

"Beautiful family," Doris said with a smile. "You and the younger boy look a lot like your mother. Has anyone told you that?"

"Yes," she said with a smile. "I've heard that."

As Dana put the photo back in her billfold, Doris released a soft sigh. "I can't add much more to the story, but if you're really intent on following up, I can tell you where to look."

Dana looked up at the older woman. "Oh?"

"When it first happened, it was all over the local paper here in Maryville, and I bet it might have been an even bigger deal in your mama's hometown." Doris patted her hand. "If you want to know everything that happened, you need to get yourself to the library and look up those newspapers."

Chapter Six

"Good God." Doyle looked up at his sister with a stunned expression. "I figured whatever had happened to Mom must have been pretty bad, but—"

"I know." Dana caught her brother's hand and gave it a comforting squeeze. "It was hard to hear."

"It's hard to believe. Mom was the most levelheaded person I've ever known. For her to go off the deep end and try to steal someone else's baby—I can't even picture her doing anything like that."

"She'd just lost a child. And she was little more than a child herself." Dana had spent the past thirty minutes alone in the waiting room just down the hall from her brother's room, preparing herself to tell him what Doris Kingsley had revealed. She'd had trouble herself reconciling the picture the nurse had painted of her mother and her own memories of Tallie Massey, a strong-minded, kindhearted woman of good sense and honorable intentions. "I don't know how she would have reacted in such a situation. We never knew her at that age or in those circumstances."

"I wish she was still here." Doyle passed a hand over his face, his eyes dark with regrets. "I wish she could tell us what happened."

"Doris Kingsley thinks we should let it go. Stop trying to find answers. She said digging up bones wouldn't make us feel any better."

Doyle gave her a knowing look. "She doesn't know you."

"Or you."

Doyle looked down at his cast-encased leg. "Yeah, if I can ever get out of this damned hospital."

"Tomorrow," said a voice from the doorway. Dana turned to find Laney standing there, holding a brown paper bag in one hand and a tablet-style device in the other. "I brought food and reading material."

Doyle went for the bag of food first, to no one's surprise. Dana gave Laney a hug and moved so that she could have the chair beside the bed. "Tomorrow, for sure?"

"That's what the doctor says," Doyle said with a grumble. "I don't know why they want to keep me around. I've been trying to give them reason to kick me out, but they're awfully patient with me."

"He's been a bear." Laney gave him a stern look. "I'm beginning to rethink this whole engagement."

Doyle touched her face. "Don't do that. I'll be good."

She kissed his palm. "It'll take worse behavior than a little surliness for you to get rid of me."

"Oh, God, they're at it again." Another voice came from the doorway, this time belonging to one of Doyle's detectives. Ivy Calhoun, Dana remembered. With her was a taller, more slender woman with light brown hair and intelligent blue eyes.

Ivy introduced her as Rachel Hammond, a friend. "We had lunch here in town, so I thought I'd drop by to see how the chief's doing."

"Suck-up," Doyle said with a smile.

Ivy grinned. "I'm bucking for chief of detectives."

"Yeah, well, you'll have to take that up with Antoine." Doyle nodded toward Rachel. "Dana, you should talk to Rachel about looking up those old newspapers you were talking about. She used to be a librarian."

Rachel Hammond's eyes lit up at the mention of her former job. "You need help finding something at the library?"

"Oh, Lord, you spoke the magic words," Ivy said with a grin.

"Specifically some old newspapers from about thirty-seven years ago," Dana said. Doris Kingsley had remembered the year, though not the month, that Tallie Cumberland had been a patient here at Maryville Mercy Hospital.

She'd have been seventeen at the time, Dana thought. Within two years of losing her son, she'd married Dana's father and gotten pregnant with Dana herself.

But what had her life been like between losing her son and meeting the man she'd marry?

"I can take you to the library whenever you like," Rachel said, eagerness evident in her voice. "Or maybe I can introduce you to some primary sources."

"She means people, not books," Ivy translated in a dry drawl.

"Primary sources would be terrific," Dana said quickly. "When do you get off work?"

"I'm the CEO of my company," Rachel said with a smile. "I make my own hours. I can go whenever you like."

"Now?"

"Sure." Rachel's smile reminded Dana of a kid who'd just been let out of school for the summer. "I need a ride, though. I left my car at the office."

"No problem. I'll drive you back to the office

when we're done." Dana waggled her fingers at the others. "See you later."

As she and Rachel walked to the hospital parking deck, Dana briefly outlined what she was looking for, without using names or going into minute detail. "I'm not sure of the month, but I'm pretty sure of the year."

"You're talking about Tallie Cumberland, aren't you?"

Dana stopped in the middle of the corridor. "You've heard the story, too?"

"Well, yeah. I live in Bitterwood, you know."

"It was a bit before your time."

"Only by a few years. And let me tell you, it was a big deal in my neighborhood, because the way I heard it, the family whose child was nearly abducted were Very Important People." The emphasis Rachel put on the last three words made Dana's chest ache. Her poor mother, she thought, young, poor and swallowed up by grief, forced to withstand the onslaught of people with power and wealth who could, without question, ruin her. No wonder she had fled Bitterwood and not looked back.

Not looked back, that was, until she'd returned here fifteen years ago on her first real vacation in years.

Why had she come here? What had she hoped to find?

The child she thought had been stolen from her? Had she still believed her baby was alive, after so much time and distance from her original grief?

"It can be a pain to get access to newspaper archives from that far back," Rachel told her as they drove out of the hospital parking deck. "But I know a guy at the *Bitterwood Town Crier*—he's been there for over forty years. Started working on the presses and eventually made his way up to reporter, then editor. If anyone on earth can tell you everything you need to know about the Tallie Cumberland story, it's T. J. Spencer."

They were back in Bitterwood within twenty minutes. By then, it was nearly lunchtime, and Rachel suggested they offer to take T.J. out to lunch. "He eats most days at Ledbetter's Diner because he can walk there from the paper," Rachel said. "But I happen to know that T.J. fancies himself a man of the world, and there's a really good Lebanese place that's opened in Purgatory near The Gates, that new detective agency where Ivy's husband works."

T. J. Spencer turned out to be a tall, barrel-chested man in his mid-sixties. His thinning red hair was liberally streaked with silver, and his face was lined by the years, but he had a masculinity and vitality that reminded Dana of her father. She liked him immediately and liked him even more a half hour later, when he'd filled in a lot of the gaps in what she knew about her mother's ordeal three decades earlier.

"It's a shame, how people treated that poor girl," T.J. said with a shake of his head as he dipped a sliver of pita bread into the baba ghanoush he'd ordered as an appetizer. "She never did tell anyone who the father was. I hear it was a surprise she was pregnant at all—she'd been the only one of the Cumberlands around these parts who'd managed to stay out of trouble for any length of time."

"Did you know her?" Dana asked.

"Not really. I went to school with her uncle Royce, whose claim to fame around here was that he ran a big moonshine still in an old barn off Pepperwood Road, but I guess you'd say the Cumberlands and I ran in different circles." He didn't sound apologetic, just matter-of-fact. "There were a ton of those kids in these parts back then. Before what happened, I mean."

"And afterward?" Dana asked.

T.J.'s eyes narrowed. "Bitterwood became a bad place for Cumberlands."

"In what way?"

"Well, for instance, a few days after Tallie tried to steal the baby, Royce's still blew up. And when he rebuilt it, it blew up again. Cumberlands were being rounded up by local law goin' and comin', for stuff they deserved to be arrested for, sure, but also a few things that seemed pretty petty, if you want my opinion."

"So the Cumberlands figured they'd worn out their welcome around here?" Rachel asked.

"I reckon that's exactly how it went."

"And it was all because of what my mother did?"

T.J. gave her a long, considering look. "I suppose it wasn't so much what your mama did as who she did it to."

"You know who the baby's parents were?"

"I do," T.J. answered with a nod. "Paul and Nina Hale."

Next to Dana, Rachel reacted with a soft gasp. "You're kidding."

"I take it that's bad?" Dana guessed.

Rachel blew out a long breath. "Well, yeah, since about half of anything worth owning in Bitterwood belongs to either his family or hers. My family was comfortably well-off, but these people could have bought and sold everything we owned twice over and never even given it a thought."

Money equals power, Dana thought, *especially when the opponent has no assets at all.* Her mother had messed with the wrong family.

"How'd they manage to keep their names out of the papers?" Dana asked. "I mean, several people have told me the story, but you're the first person who could name the family, which means it never got written up. Did they pay off the newspaper?"

T.J. laughed. "Not exactly."

"Nina's father is Pete Sutherland," Rachel said, as if that would mean something to Dana.

It didn't. "And Pete Sutherland is?"

T.J. grinned, though there wasn't a lot of humor in his expression. "Pete Sutherland is my boss. He owns and publishes the *Bitterwood Town Crier*."

"IT STILL DOESN'T explain how he managed to keep his daughter's name out of the Maryville newspaper." Dana's voice sounded equal parts excited and frustrated over the phone.

Nix zipped his leather jacket and pondered what she'd told him. The Sutherlands and Hales were Bitterwood's version of the Morgans and the Rockefellers. Smaller scale in terms of wealth, of course, but their level of influence was formidable. The Hales owned land and resort properties from Chattanooga to Cumberland, Maryland, choosing to live in Bitterwood for precisely the reason half its population longed to get away— its quiet, out-of-the-way seclusion.

Nix supposed the Sutherlands stuck around the little town for much the same reason, long after Pete's father had sold several newspapers back in print's heyday for a fortune and invested his earnings in oil and mining interests. Old Pete was a Bitterwood celebrity of sorts, an old-fashioned newspaperman who still liked to have a little ink on his hands. He might be rich, but he didn't put on airs, taking delight in his Appalachian roots and his reverence for the area's history.

Hell, Nix had always liked the old coot himself. But he'd never crossed the man, so he'd never had occasion to see Mr. Sutherland's darker side. Assuming a darker side even existed.

"What do you propose to do about it, now that you have that information?" he asked Dana, putting the phone on speaker and setting it on the bed beside him while he pulled on his boots.

"Well, that's why I'm calling you," she answered. "I considered trying to meet the Hales to get their sides of the story, but Rachel Hammond seemed to think contacting them would be a bad idea at this point. And since she grew up amongst their ilk, I figured I should defer to her wisdom on the subject."

Nix grinned at her word choices. "Probably smart. But if you're hoping I can get you any closer to the town muckety-mucks, you're out of luck. I'm from Cherokee Cove, not Edgewood. I have a feeling there were probably some Nixes run out of town right along with the Cumberlands back in the day."

"Believe me, your redneck roots are what I'm

banking on. I'd like to talk to some folks in Cherokee Cove."

Oh, no, he thought. *Bad idea. Very bad idea.* Especially considering how much she apparently looked like her mother, if the whispers he'd been hearing since she came to town were anything to go by. Cumberlands had become easy scapegoats for all the problems people in his little neck of the woods had suffered over the ensuing years. They haunted Cherokee Cove even today, long after the last Cumberland had pulled up stakes and headed for more welcoming parts of the state.

"Listen, we should talk about this, but not now. I'm following a different lead, and besides, taking a cop into Cherokee Cove isn't the way to get information."

"But you're one of them."

"Not when I'm wearing the badge," he answered firmly. Which was why he wasn't going to be wearing the badge today, at least not where anyone in town could see it. "Tell you what. I'll call you later, when I get some time."

"Fine." The tightness in her voice made him wince with guilt, but he reminded himself that she'd gone on her hospital detective jaunt without consulting him, and the guilt passed. If he found out anything that might answer their questions about who had tried to kill the chief, he'd tell her. But until then, he was a cop on a case and she was, fancy federal badge or not, a family member of the victim, in town on vacation. She'd just have to be patient.

He should have known patience wasn't one of Dana Massey's virtues.

THE SMALL COMMUNITY of Cherokee Cove, on the northern slope of Smoky Ridge, lay nestled in a shadowy, wooded valley in the side of the mountain. There was only one road in or out, which probably explained why Dana didn't manage to get twenty yards past the first house before people started coming out into their yards to watch her drive past.

She ignored their unsmiling gazes and drove on until she reached a small cluster of buildings that seemed to be the sum total of the community's business district. There was a tiny post office, a hardware store and a small grocery on one side of the road. On the other side stood a small brick church with a white steeple. Nowhere to park in front of either the post office or the store, she noted with surprise. She turned off the road and parked in the gravel lot next to the little brick church.

By the time she'd locked her car door and turned back toward the main street, people had come out of the buildings to stand on porches and sidewalks, watching her approach. Nobody moved. Nobody smiled, either. There were men and women, old and young, all watching her through narrowed eyes as she neared the dusty walking path that led to the small grocery store.

"Hello," she said, quelling the urge to check the ammunition in the pistol holstered beneath her windbreaker. "My name is Dana Massey—"

"We know who you are." A thin man in his sixties stepped forward from the porch of the grocery store. He was dressed in jeans and a plaid shirt, his clothes clean but his shoes crusted with dried mud. He wore a faded baseball cap with *Riddle Brothers Tractor* embroidered in blue on the front. The bill shadowed his weathered face, making it hard to read the intent in his eyes.

"Do you know why I'm here?" she asked.

"You're nosing around in something you ought to let lie." That was a woman, speaking from the concrete stoop in front of the post office. She was possibly even older than the man with the baseball cap, her silver hair wispy and fluttering in the breeze. She wore a cotton house dress beneath a thick wool cardigan, with flat canvas shoes on her small feet. She couldn't have been more than five feet tall, but her advancing years seemed to have toughened her into steel and leather, all muscles and sinew. Here was a woman who'd worked hard all her life, and it showed.

"I want to know more about my mother." She

had to assume, from the rapid-fire spread of information about her arrival, that the people of the community had already known she was in Bitterwood. She'd been asking a lot of questions about her mother over the past couple of days. In a town this small, it wouldn't have taken long for word to get around.

"Your mama brought trouble here. That's all you need to know." The woman turned and went back into the post office.

But nobody else moved away. If anything, they'd formed a phalanx, as if to wall the town off from her presence.

"What do you think she did to you?" Dana asked, frustration rising in her chest on a swell of anger. "She was a girl who lost a baby. She didn't kill him."

"You don't know anything, city girl." The speaker's voice came from behind her. She turned quickly and found herself face-to-face with a bearded man around her own age. He wasn't any taller than she was, but he was built like a barn, with broad shoulders, a chest the size of a rain barrel and massive arms and thighs. There was a little flab in his gut, but the rest of him looked hard and thick, like a football lineman.

He stood close enough that, for the first time since she'd parked in front of the store, she felt physically threatened. She might be able to outrun him, but if he got physical, she didn't think she could outfight him.

And the last thing she wanted to do, in the middle of this increasingly hostile crowd, was to pull her gun on him, even to save her own life.

"I'm really not here for trouble," she stated, backing toward her car. The man's face cracked into a narrow-eyed smile, but he didn't move after her.

Reaching the edge of the church's gravel parking lot, she turned toward her car. And swallowed a curse.

The Chevy's driver's-side tires were both flat.

She didn't know whether to be scared or mad as hell.

As she turned back to confront the gathered crowd, the rumble of an engine filtered past the low murmurs of the people watching her. Dana looked down the road, trying to locate the source of the noise. She saw several in the small crowd turn their heads, as well.

Around the curve just visible about fifty yards away, a motorcycle zoomed into view, its engine noise increasing to a loud growl. The driver was dressed in black, from a worn leather jacket to tight-fitting black jeans that hugged his muscular legs from his narrow hips to his boots. The bike was an old Harley-Davidson Sportster, similar to one her father had owned, all shiny black and chrome. It slowed to a crawl as it reached the clump of onlookers, rolling to a stop in front of Dana.

The rider flipped up the visor of his helmet, revealing Walker Nix's coffee-colored eyes. Dana felt a flood of relief so powerful it made her knees tremble.

Nix's gaze slid past her to take in the state of her car, then whipped back to meet her surprised stare. The look he gave her was equal parts regret and resignation.

"Get on the back," he said, "and let's get you the hell out of here."

Chapter Seven

Nix couldn't say why, exactly, he had kept his grandfather's cabin a few miles up the mountain from Cherokee Cove. It wasn't much to look at, inside or out, and as recently as twenty years earlier, the place hadn't even had indoor plumbing. But some of his best memories of growing up in the Smokies had happened in that cabin, and when his grandfather died and left the place to him, he'd ignored his father's advice and kept it.

Of course, when he'd left the marine corps and moved back to Tennessee to finally assess the condition the cabin was in, he'd been tempted to apologize to his father. But he'd quickly seen that the cabin's bones were solid, and little by little over the past five years, he'd begun to turn it into a home.

He found himself watching Dana's face as she took in the rustic trappings of the old cabin, from the rough-hewn rocking chairs on the dusty wood-slat porch to the deer antlers that lined the plain oak mantel over the sooty fireplace.

"You hunt much?" she asked.

He shook his head. "No. Not a lot of time or need. There are people around these parts who hunt to eat. I leave the wildlife to them." In fact, he thought, he'd gone into Cherokee Cove to talk to one of those people, but Dana's dilemma had derailed his plans, at least temporarily.

"Inherited?" she guessed.

Nodding, he waved toward the sofa, one of the newer pieces in the place. "I'll call Brantley's Garage to go pick up your car."

"I didn't leave the keys," she said, her voice more subdued than he liked. Her showdown with the crowd back in Cherokee Cove must have shaken her more than he'd realized.

"We'll meet them down the road."

She sat on the sofa, watching as he pulled a small phone directory from the drawer of the table where he kept the phone. "Won't that mean driving back through there again?"

"Are you afraid to go back?"

The look she shot his way was sharp enough to cut. "No, I'd just prefer not to have to shoot anybody today."

He stifled a grin.

"And I really don't enjoy riding a motorcycle without a helmet."

"We'll take my truck." He dialed the number of Brantley's Garage and talked to Wally, telling him where Dana had parked her car. Wally agreed to meet them at Parson's Crossing, where Cherokee Cove Road intersected with Parson Hollow Road.

As he hung up, Dana asked, "What were you doing in Cherokee Cove anyway?"

"Following up another lead."

"You didn't mention your other lead was in Cherokee Cove when I asked you to take me there."

"No, I didn't."

"Who did you come to see in Cherokee Cove?" she asked, not deterred by his attempt to end the conversation.

"You're not officially on this case, you know," he said.

"Do I have to call my brother?" she asked, a glint of humor in her eye.

"You'd really play that card?"

Her only answer was a slight twitch of her eyebrow.

"Fine. I came here to see a woman."

Her face reddened. "Oh."

"Do you want to tag along?"

Her eyes narrowed, making him grin. She flattened her lips to a thin line and shot him a hard look. "Sure, I'm up for it," she said through gritted teeth.

"Let's just hope I am," he muttered as he grabbed his truck keys and headed outside.

THE WOMAN IN question was a wiry, dark-haired woman in her late twenties who watched the truck's approach through narrowed eyes. Her wary expression cleared when she got a better look at the vehicle, and she went back to what she'd been doing when they'd come over the hill, her hoe chopping up the rocky soil of what looked to be a fallow garden in front of her small wooden cabin.

She was a natural sort of pretty, with lots of curly black hair and a spattering of freckles across her tanned face. She gave a nod of hello to Nix and then, resting the hoe on the ground, she turned her curious gaze on Dana. "Hello."

Movement on the porch behind her caught Dana's eye before she could respond. There was a little boy rocking back and forth on a homemade rocking horse that had been carved from pine logs. He couldn't be more than two or three years old, and the solemn gray eyes that stared back at her from a lightly freckled face were just like the woman's, the color of the cloudy sky overhead—gray with a hint of gunmetal along the edges.

"Briar Blackwood, this is Dana Massey. Dana,

this is Briar." Nix moved past Briar and took the porch steps in one quick bound, reaching down to the little boy on the rocking horse. The baby grinned up at him and lifted his arms, rewarded with a swooping swing to Nix's hip. "And this," Nix added, "is my man Logan."

"My son," Briar added, unnecessarily.

"Nice to meet you both," Dana said.

"Briar's a dispatcher."

"For the police department?"

"Police and fire," Briar corrected with a little smile. "It's a small town."

She had a strong accent, Dana noticed, as thick as those of the people she'd spoken to on Cherokee Cove Road outside the post office. She supposed Briar's cabin was still in Cherokee Cove, but she and Nix had gone off the main paved road not far from where they'd met Wally from the garage to hand over Dana's keys, traveling a narrow, winding road into the woods for almost a mile before they'd reached this small clearing where Briar and her son lived.

"Starting a garden?" Dana waved toward the hoe and the broken ground.

"Yeah. It's finally gotten warm enough that I can start putting stuff out for the summer without worrying about a deep freeze."

"What do you grow?" Dana asked as Nix

crossed to where they stood, still bouncing Logan on one hip.

"Tomatoes, green beans, okra, squash, peppers—pretty much anything we can put up in the freezer or can," she answered. "Do you garden?"

"I did when I was a kid," Dana answered. "But I live in an apartment in Atlanta now. Not really much time or space for gardening."

"That's right. You're a deputy U.S. marshal." Briar's lips curved into a toothy smile. "Hell, you might have brought in some of my kinfolk. I come from a dicey bunch."

"Apparently so do I," Dana murmured.

Nix's lips twitched as he caught her comment. "Speaking of your dicey kinfolk, Briar, I heard that one of your cousins is a member of the Blue Ridge Infantry."

Briar turned to look at Nix, her expression cautious. "You mean Blake?"

"That's the one."

"He hasn't been around here in months. We don't want his kind of trouble."

"I hear he was up around Purgatory the other day."

Briar looked genuinely surprised. "He's an idiot, then."

"Friends of mine think he might be trying to recruit folks from around here. With the economy like it is and some of the stuff coming out of Washington—"

"I won't say there aren't some fool-minded people around here who'd fall for that kind of sales pitch, but I haven't heard anything about it, and I generally hear just about everything that goes on in these parts. Like just a few minutes ago, I got a phone call tellin' me that there was a Cumberland in Cherokee Cove, like I was supposed to run and take cover." She slanted a look toward Dana. "I reckon they meant you?"

"People there were really not happy to see me."

"No, I don't suppose they were." Briar nodded toward the cabin. "Y'all come on inside. It's time for Logan's nap, and I've got a pitcher of iced tea in the fridge." She didn't wait for them to agree, just plucked her son out of Nix's arms and started up the porch steps to the cabin.

Nix rested his hand against the small of Dana's back and gave her a light nudge forward. She pretended to ignore the quivering response of her skin to the heat of his touch and followed Briar into the cabin.

Inside, the place was small but neat. *Efficient* was the better word, Dana thought. Everything in the house seemed to be there for use rather than show, from the old-fashioned juice press on the kitchen counter to the row of colorful root-vegetable bins lined up on one side of the tidy kitchen, full of onions, potatoes and turnips. Daylight seeped in the windows through a prism of color—one-and two-quart Mason jars full of pickled cucumbers and okra, deep red tomatoes and the bright jewel tones of peaches, blueberries and strawberries, all lining every available windowsill and shelf in the place.

"I don't have a whole lot of root-cellar space," Briar explained as she returned from putting her son down for a nap and spotted Dana looking around the place in wonder. "I have to put the jars up high, where Logan can't reach them, or he's likely to pry a jar open and start munching."

Dana grinned at the picture Briar's words evoked. "My mother used to can every chance she got. She said it was relaxing. My dad always teased her about it, saying she had pioneer blood."

"He was right. Cumberlands have been in these parts since the first settlers came down from Virginia."

"Not anymore."

Briar took a deep breath through her nose, as if steadying herself for what was about to come. Dana found herself doing the same, girding herself for whatever the young woman was about to tell her.

"Your mama was the cause of that," Briar said.

Nix touched Dana's back again, his hand warm

and firm against her spine. "Why don't we sit down?" he suggested.

"You want any tea?" Briar asked as Dana sat on the small, neat sofa under a window full of Mason jars.

"No, thanks."

"Me, either." Nix sat down beside her, sticking close, as if to offer support. She wondered if she was going to need it.

Briar took the armchair across from them. "Let me start out by saying, there's many of us around here who don't think your mama was to blame for anything. That story about her killin' the baby, well, there were people who got their own benefit from lettin' that story circulate, you know what I mean? And not just some of the folks around Cherokee Cove who'd gotten sideways with the Cumberlands, either. There were others, folks who wouldn't care to step foot into this hollow, who had their own agendas for makin' sure the Cumberlands couldn't cause anyone any trouble."

"You mean the Sutherlands and Hales, don't you?" Dana asked.

Briar's eyebrows ticked upward. "How'd you find out?"

"She's a deputy U.S. marshal, remember," Nix answered for her.

"So you know your mother was found in the

basement of Maryville Mercy Hospital with Nina Hale's newborn son."

"That's what I hear."

"I think that much of the story is pretty much the truth," Briar said. "But the part about her killin' her baby? I think it's hogwash. Oh, it makes for a better story, I'll grant you. And people like drama in their stories. But when you dig through all the storytelling and get to what people really remember about Tallie Cumberland, you find out she wouldn't have harmed a bottle fly."

"That sounds a lot more like the woman who raised me than any of these other stories do," Dana agreed.

"You have to understand, long before Tallie lost her baby, the Cumberlands were trouble in these parts. Tallie's daddy was a moonshiner, her mama was prone to takin' lovers, and all three of Tallie's brothers had criminal records. Hell, her uncle Dawes Cumberland was on death row for killin' two men for their drink money in a bar down in Chattanooga. You'll hear folks around here say none of the Cumberlands is worth a damn, and for the most part, they'd be right. But your mama was an exception."

"You're too young to have known her," Dana said.

"I am," Briar agreed. "But my mama knew

her. And she's the one who told me not to listen to what people said about Tallie Cumberland. Because they didn't know what they were talking about."

Even though Dana had known the stories about her mother couldn't be true, it was a relief to hear someone else in town agree. "I'd love to speak to your mother."

A hint of pain darkened Briar's eyes. "I'd love to talk to her, too."

"Briar's mother died of cancer three years ago," Nix murmured.

"I'm sorry."

"Me, too." Briar took a long, slow breath. "You know, when I was a kid, I think I was the only girl around these parts who was friends with a Cumberland. My friend Nadine was a distant relative of your mama's, from a group of cousins who hadn't even lived here in decades. Her family moved back to this area after her dad lost his job in Memphis. They lived south of here a ways, but we went to the same school in town. I used to invite her to come to my house, but she refused to step foot in Cherokee Cove. She was afraid the folk around here might try to kill her just for being who she was."

"That's crazy," Dana said.

"Welcome to Cherokee Cove," Nix murmured.

He looked at Briar. "Nadine's family didn't stick around long, did they? I don't remember much about them."

"You were already in high school, and all of their kids were younger," Briar explained. "And no, they didn't last long. They moved back to Memphis within a couple of years."

"Did all the Cumberlands leave when my mother left?"

"Within a year of that time, yes," Briar said with a nod. "And who could blame them? *Cumberland* might as well have been a swearword around here. Any wildfire, blizzard, rock slide, tree blight or fish kill in these parts seemed to get blamed on the Cumberlands, long after they'd moved away. I guess people thought they cursed the ground before they left or something."

"And you haven't talked to Nadine since she left?"

"I still talk to her, sometimes. On the phone, mostly. She and her family never came back here again, especially not after—" Briar stopped suddenly, her eyes narrowing as she looked at Dana.

"Not after what?" Dana asked.

"Briar—" Nix looked at the younger woman, his expression hard to read. Dana suddenly realized there was a whole conversation going on between the two of them, without a word being spoken.

"What don't you want me to hear?" she asked Nix.

He looked at her. "I don't want you to hear rumors that can't be proved."

"I'm old enough to know the difference," she snapped.

His nostrils flared, but he sat back, giving a little wave of his hand as if to tell Briar to proceed.

"Nix is right," Briar said. "What I'm telling you is nothing but rumors. And you know how reliable rumors around here are."

"Understood."

"The last time I saw Nadine in person was fifteen years ago. February eighteenth."

It took Dana a moment to do the math. "That's the day my parents died."

Briar nodded. "Nadine didn't show up for school the next day. Or the day after that. So I talked my mama into taking me to see her."

Dana had a feeling she knew where Briar's story was going. "Let me guess. They had moved away without any warning?"

"No, they were there." Briar glanced at Nix, as if needing his permission to continue. Dana glanced at Nix and found him looking not at Briar but at her, his expression bleak.

He knows, she thought. *Whatever it is Briar's trying to tell me, he knows.*

She looked at Briar again. "But?"

"But they were in the middle of loading up a moving truck and getting the hell out of town," she answered. "They said it wasn't safe to be anywhere near Bitterwood if you're a Cumberland."

"Because of what happened to my parents?"

"Nadine told me that your mama had asked questions about what happened at the hospital in Maryville. Her daddy said she'd stepped on the wrong toes and paid for it."

Dana shook her head, not wanting to hear the rest, even as she knew she had to know.

"That's enough," Nix said.

"No," Dana managed to say in a low growl. "Tell me the rest. What did Nadine tell you about my parents' accident?"

Briar looked as if she wanted to be anywhere but here in this little cabin, face-to-face with Dana. But she lifted her chin, finally, raised her gaze to meet Dana's and spoke. "Nadine said that the Sutherlands and Hales killed her to keep folks from finding out the truth about her baby."

"What truth?"

"Everybody in the Cumberland family believes that it wasn't Tallie's baby that died that day in Maryville but the Hales' baby. And it was the Hales who stole Tallie's baby for themselves." Briar's eyes darkened. "They killed your parents because they'd come back to town asking questions about the baby."

Chapter Eight

The ride back to Bitterwood wasn't exactly a silent affair, thanks to the rattle of the old truck's engine, but Dana didn't appear inclined to hash out all she'd heard from Briar Blackwood. Nix had seen the way she had taken in everything Briar had said, her quick mind at work behind those green eyes, weighing facts and speculation to figure out what to believe and what to discard.

Taking everything Briar had said at face value was dangerous. Even Briar had reiterated, after dropping the bombshell about the accident, that the only source of her information was Nadine, who in turn had gotten her information from family members who were less than reliable.

"I understand," Dana had said, but Nix had seen the speculation in her eyes. She was a woman who made her living solving mysteries, in a way. Not in the investigative sense, perhaps, but a deputy U.S. marshal had to be able to sift through rumors and innuendo to find the facts that could lead her to the fugitive she sought.

He was curious to find out what she'd concluded.

She remained quiet as they cooled their heels in the waiting area at Brantley's Garage to get an update on her car. Nix took the chair next to her and spent a few minutes pretending to read a car magazine before he tossed the magazine aside and turned to look at her.

"What are you thinking?"

Dana's gaze flicked up to meet his. "That is such a girlie thing to ask."

He grinned. "I'm a sensitive guy."

"I'm thinking that we skipped lunch and I'm hungry."

"We can walk across the street to the diner if you want."

"How much longer do you think it's going to take to get an answer on my car?" She arched her neck to see over the window that looked into the garage's service bays. She gave a small start as Wally, the mechanic who'd picked up her car, suddenly appeared in the window and flashed her a grin.

He came through the door into the waiting area. "We've got you all fixed up, but I had to replace two of your tires. Someone did a job on them."

"Slashed?" Nix asked.

Wally nodded. "And in a church parking lot of all places." He shook his head with dismay. "I had some good-quality refurbished tires, so that's what I put on for you. If you want a new set, I'll have to order them for you, or you might try the tire store over in Maryville."

Dana pulled out her wallet and withdrew a debit card. "Thank you for the quick service."

Wally took the card. "My pleasure."

While they waited for Wally to put the payment through the computer, Nix leaned closer to Dana, lowering his voice. "Still want to grab something at the diner?"

She seemed to think about it for a moment, then shook her head. "I'd rather go back to Doyle's. I've had enough ogling from strangers for one day."

Nix felt a flutter of disappointment and gave himself a mental kick. What did he think a dinner together would have been, even if she'd agreed to it? A date?

Don't be an idiot, Nix.

"I wouldn't mind company for dinner, though," she added quietly, her gaze slanting toward him briefly. "I'm not a great cook, but I can put together something edible. Want to tag along?"

"Sure," he said before he could stop himself.

He followed her car back to Doyle's, spending

most of the short trip trying to talk himself out of the sudden swell of anticipation chasing through his chest. *It's dinner, man. Not a chance to score.*

She seemed to expect him to help her put dinner together, so he followed her into her brother's small kitchen and started looking for easy options. The chief had several cans of vegetables, so he picked out a few he liked and showed them to Dana for her approval. She nodded at the turnip greens and canned corn, motioning for him to grab a pan and start heating them on the stove.

She found a box of microwavable fish fillets in the freezer and showed it to Nix. "How far the boy from the beach has fallen," she drawled, making him smile.

"We *are* a little landlocked up here," he defended the chief.

"You have lakes, don't you? He can't go catch his own?"

"He's been busy, you know, defending the town and winning the girl."

"I do like Laney," she said. "She's a way better woman than I ever thought he'd go for. His taste in women hasn't always been so discriminating."

"Laney's good people," he agreed. "You met her family, didn't you?"

"Just barely. We've all been a little preoccupied since Doyle's accident." She opened the box of fillets and pulled out the two frozen slabs of tilapia. "Fish okay with you?"

"Fish is fine with me." He searched the pantry for spices to perk up the canned vegetables, settling on the staples—onion powder, garlic powder, black pepper and salt. "Do you do much cooking at home?"

"There are a dozen great restaurants in walking distance from my apartment." She shot him a wry smile.

"I guess you stay too busy to indulge in domesticity?"

She gave him a sidelong glance as she punched the buttons on the microwave to start it. "You prefer your women to cook, clean and pop out babies?"

Not at this moment, he thought. "Only if that's what they want. Just call me an enlightened hillbilly."

Smiling, she turned to face him, flattening one hand on the counter and putting the other on her hip. "I don't mind cooking when I have time and the resources. I'm actually pretty clean by nature. And I guess if my life had turned out differently, I would have liked having babies, too."

"No time for marriage and family?"

"No time, no opportunity." She shrugged and turned back to look at the microwave. "In my job, most of the men I meet are either already married, not in the market for a work relationship or fugitive felons."

"You must love your job, then."

"I do. Mostly."

"Mostly?"

She sighed deeply. "My bosses made me take this vacation because I get so focused on my job that it's probably not healthy. Doyle thinks I focus on the job because it keeps me from dealing with other facets of life."

"Like husbands and babies?"

She shrugged. "Maybe he's right. I have my reasons."

And there she went, dangling a mystery in front of him. He bit. "Such as?"

She shot him a quelling look. "They're personal."

"Well, yeah, I figured that. But you're the one who brought it up."

Her eyes narrowing, she looked back at him. "What about you? I didn't see any signs of wedded bliss back at your cabin, either."

Touché, he thought. "No, I'm still single."

"You and Briar seem close. Logan obviously adores you."

"Briar?" He shook his head. "That'd be too much like dating my sister."

"You're not gay, are you?"

"No." Remembering what he'd been picturing

while riding with her thighs wrapped around his on the back of the Harley, he stifled a grin.

"Considering the priesthood?"

He laughed aloud that time. "Definitely not."

The microwave gave a ding, and she turned her attention back to the fish while he stirred the vegetables, which had begun to bubble on the stove eye. A few minutes later, he dished servings of turnip greens and corn onto the two plates she held out for him, and they carried their meal to the small kitchen table.

"Not sure what Doyle has in the way of beverages," she warned as she opened the refrigerator.

"Water is fine for me," he told her. He got up and retrieved the glasses from the cabinet to the right of the sink.

She closed the refrigerator, mumbling something about needing to go grocery shopping, and took the glass Nix handed her. Filling the glasses with ice and water from the refrigerator dispenser, they settled down to their meal.

The fish wasn't half-bad, to Nix's surprise, though he was like Briar in one regard—he liked to know where his food was coming from. He didn't have a garden of his own, but between his mother and Briar, he usually had enough fresh from the garden fruits and vegetables to get by. He went fishing when he could, keeping and cleaning his catch. He didn't hunt much anymore, but a single deer could keep him in venison steaks for months.

"You should tell your brother to make friends with some of these hill folks," he told Dana as he finished up the food on his plate. "They'd probably be happy to keep him stocked up with fresh meat and vegetables."

"Ah, but then he'd have to cook instead of stick things in the microwave," she said with a smile. "Clearly, you have much to learn about my brother."

Nix shrugged. "His loss."

Her smile faded. "I didn't mean to make light of the offer."

"I guess your experience with local hospitality hasn't exactly been a good one."

"Today wasn't great," she admitted. "But Briar was lovely. And everyone at the station has been a big help to me." She pushed her plate away, biting her lower lip. He was beginning to recognize what that expression meant—there was something she wanted to say, but she wasn't sure how to say it.

"Everyone was a big help, but…?"

"I'm not sure that helpfulness will stand when I tell them what I want."

He had a sinking feeling he knew what she was going to ask. But he couldn't blame her. If he'd been in her position, he'd want to know the same answers. "You want to look at the case file on your parents' accident."

"Wouldn't you?"

"Yeah, I would. And I'll help you find the files."

Her smile was like sunshine breaking through the clouds on a rainy day. He gave himself a mental kick for even thinking such a corny thought, but he wasn't immune to the effects of that smile. He felt instantly hot all over and antsy to get closer to her. The tiny table between them suddenly seemed like an enormous obstacle.

She stood from the table and he moved with her as she started toward the cabin door. "So, how hard is it going to be to find the files?"

He caught up with her before she reached the middle of the front room, catching her arm. "You want to go now?"

She gave him a puzzled look. "Well, yeah."

"It's well after five. The file room will have been shut down for the night. Support staff gets to go home regular hours."

"Don't you have to go back to the office and type up a report of your day or something?" She pulled him with her toward the door.

He tugged her back to him, apparently catching her off guard, for she stumbled into him, her breasts flattening against his chest. All the air seemed to leak right out of his lungs as she clutched the front of his jacket to steady herself, staring up at him with those bright green eyes.

He made himself let her go, even though every nerve in his body was screaming for him to pull her closer. "If we go tonight, I'll have to explain why we need the key to the file room. People will ask a lot of questions we don't necessarily want to answer yet. If we wait until morning, when the file room will already be open for the day, I can look for the files myself without anyone but the file-room clerk having to know what I want or why."

Frustration darkened her eyes, but she gave a nod. "Okay. You're right." Her shoulders slumped a little in defeat. "But I guess you still need to go file a report?"

"You want me to go?"

Her gaze snapped up to his again. "No. I don't."

"Then it can wait until morning, too." He nodded toward the sofa, which was angled so that it sat right in front of the fireplace. The temperature outside had dropped with the setting sun, leaving a distinct chill in the air, even inside the heated cabin. He nodded at the dark hearth. "How about a fire?"

"Sounds good. Do you know how to start it?"

"You are such a city slicker." He found logs in the wood bin next to the fireplace and got a fire going within a couple of minutes. Dana scooted closer, stretching her hands out toward the heat of the flames.

"Nice," she murmured.

He looked up from his crouch and felt a flipping sensation in his chest. The glow of the fire seemed to illuminate her from the inside, transforming her into a creature of light. Her auburn hair crackled with radiance and her skin glowed like burnished gold. Flames reflected in her green eyes as she looked down at him, the hint of a smile on her lips.

He rose slowly, testing his resistance and finding it weak. "Fire becomes you."

The smile spread. "What a courtly thing to say, Detective."

He couldn't stop himself from touching the lock of hair dangling against her cheek. "Are you making fun of me, Marshal?"

She shook her head. "No. I don't mind a little courtliness."

"Mama raised me to be a gentleman." And his daddy had raised him to raise hell. But he kept that part to himself.

"Does your mother still live around here?" She eased away from his touch without being unkind about it, settling on the sofa. She patted the seat next to her, and he sat before he answered.

"She lives not far from the church. The one where your tires were slashed." He waited for her to ask the obvious question. When she didn't, he continued. "She wasn't in the crowd today."

"I didn't assume she was." Dana kept her gaze focused on the fire. He couldn't tell if she was speaking the truth or just saying what she had for his benefit. "What about your dad?"

"He wasn't in the crowd, either."

She made a face. "Not what I meant."

"My dad has very little patience for superstition." He shook his head. "How he lives with my mother, I'm not sure, but they've been together for nearly forty years."

"You must see a lot of them, living so close." Dana sounded wistful as she turned to gaze at the fire.

"Not as much as my mother would like," he admitted. "But yeah. I try to go by the house once a week, at least. Mama worries about my job and Dad worries that I'm becoming a psychotic loner. You know, parents."

He regretted his flip remark about the same time Dana's expression froze with pain.

"I'm sorry," he said softly. "That was *not* a very courtly thing to say."

She managed a smile, but there was sadness at its heart. "When you're young, all you can think about is getting out of the house and making your own way. But under all that radical independence, there's this safety net you know is going to keep you from falling too hard or too far. And when that net gets ripped out from under you—" She pressed her mouth together as if saying the rest of the words might break her apart.

"You must have been pretty young when your parents died."

"I was twenty. Doyle was nineteen and David was about to turn eighteen. I really had to grow up fast after that."

"You were in college then, I guess."

"Doyle and I both were, and David was about to start. Fortunately, Mom and Dad had been big savers. It wasn't a ton of money—we still had to work through college to pay for it all, sure, but not so much that we didn't get to graduate on time."

"Did you go straight to the U.S. Marshals Service out of college?"

"Yes. I thought about trying to join the Alabama State Troopers, follow in my dad's footsteps, but Doyle talked me into the Marshals Service. He knew it would be a better fit for me."

"And the chief joined the local sheriff's department?"

"Not at first. First, he went to Mississippi and worked casino security on the coast. But that didn't really work out. And then—" She stopped again, her throat bobbing as her expression went very still and closed. "Then he quit his job, went back home to Terrebonne and took a job with the sheriff's department."

Nix had a feeling that something had happened to send the chief running home. "Where were you at that time?"

She gave him a strangely distant look, as if she didn't understand his question.

"When Doyle went back to Terrebonne, where were you working at the time?" he clarified.

"I, uh—actually, I was on leave from the Marshals Service." She looked down at her hands, which were twisting slowly in her lap. "Something had happened. Something terrible."

In the center of Nix's chest, an echo of the pain that lined her face throbbed darkly. He didn't know whether to push her to tell him the rest or let it go and change the subject. He only wanted to do whatever would erase that pain from her face.

"My brother David was different from Doyle and me," she said quietly. "He never felt the call to law enforcement. He wanted to serve people in a different way. He joined a charity group called Samaritan's Vision."

Nix's blood iced over. He'd heard of Samaritan's Vision. Almost anyone who'd watched the news ten years ago had heard of the group, after what had happened to a contingent of volunteers in Sanselmo, a conflict-plagued country on the Caribbean coast of South America.

"Dana—"

"He was in Sanselmo. He was slaughtered by one of the drug cartels that supported the rebels."

"I'm so sorry."

She sighed deeply. "So am I. David was the very best of us. Not an unkind bone in his body. Doyle and I used to joke that our parents must have found him under a rock somewhere, he was so different."

He saw moisture glistening in her eyes and wished he'd changed the subject. But maybe talking about her brother was how she worked through the pain of his loss. She looked so eager to tell him more as she turned to face him, he sat back and let her talk.

She told him about David's good grades, his cheerful attitude, the way he'd managed to be their comfort when their parents died. "He was shattered at first," she murmured with a slight smile, "but once Doyle and I were home and we were all together, it was David who helped us get past the pain and remember all the good times. He made us sit down every night for a week and tell stories of life with Mom and Dad."

"He sounds very special."

Her face crumpled, breaking his heart. "He was. And it's all kinds of wrong that he died so young, with so much life still ahead of him." She brushed away her tears, looking angry at herself for the sign of weakness.

He couldn't stop himself from touching her face, from cupping her jaw and drawing her closer. Brushing his lips to her forehead, he whispered, "I'm sorry. I'm so sorry you've lost so much in your life."

She rested her forehead against his, not pulling away. "When I saw Doyle's truck lying on its side in the road the other night, my first thought was that I'd lost him, too. That I'd lost everyone I've ever loved."

He'd seen a hint of that fear in her eyes, he remembered. Had felt its cold chill straight down to his marrow.

"He's fine," he said softly, lifting his other hand to her face.

She pulled back just far enough to gaze up at him, her eyes warm and languid with what he desperately wanted to believe was desire.

"What are we doing here?" she whispered, and it didn't sound like a rebuff. It sounded like a plea.

Slowly, deliberately, he lowered his mouth to hers, wanting just a taste, just a light brush of his lips to hers. Just enough to know what it would feel like to kiss those soft pink lips.

But of course, it didn't happen quite that way. Because the second his mouth touched hers, something exploded inside him, something incendiary, spreading flames through his body like wildfire.

Her hands clutched the front of his T-shirt, pulling him closer, her lips parted in heated response and the world spun wildly, irrevocably off its axis.

Chapter Nine

She was kissing a man she called by his last name. On some level, Dana knew that fact meant something important, that she wasn't thinking straight. But the truth was, she wasn't thinking much at all, only feeling. And what she felt was an almost palpable relief, as if this moment in time, with Nix's mouth moving relentlessly over hers, was something she'd been waiting for her whole life. It seemed to drive away the restlessness that had roamed her soul for as long as she could remember, leaving her feeling only pleasure and contentment.

If she had been thinking, not feeling, that realization would have scared her a lot more than it did.

But Nix's hands, trailing sensual fire down her throat and over her collarbone, drove anything like thought far from her mind.

His mouth migrated in soft, light kisses away from her mouth and over the curve of her jaw, settling with sweet heat on the skin just beneath her ear. He nuzzled there, a growl rumbling through his chest. "You smell good," he murmured, giving her earlobe a light nip that made her suck in a deep gasp of air.

"Thank you," she whispered.

He laughed softly, dropping his chin to the curve of her neck. His beard bristled against the sensitive flesh, sending a scattering of chill bumps across her skin. "You're welcome."

Like a little fly buzzing in the back of her mind, a desperate thread of caution tried to catch her attention. She wanted to swat it away, make it leave her alone to enjoy the delicious things Nix was doing to her with his remarkably talented hands and mouth, but she hadn't lived through a number of dangerous situations by ignoring her cautious side. With a low groan, she slid away from Nix's grasp and stood, breathing as rapidly as if she'd just run for her life. She took a few steps away from him, ending up in front of the mantel.

"Well, damn," Nix murmured.

"We can't do this." She shook her head, trying to convince her reluctant body that she was doing the right thing.

"We just did." Nix had walked up behind her, close enough that she felt the heat of his breath stir her hair.

She clenched her fists. "You know what I mean."

"You mean we shouldn't." He murmured the words against her hair, sending a hard shudder of need rumbling down her spine.

She didn't trust herself to turn around and face him. "I'm here for only a few more days. I need to concentrate on learning everything I can about the attack on my brother. I can't— I don't want to complicate everything."

She heard him take a long, deep breath. The heat of his body dissipated as he moved backward, away from where she stood. A few seconds later, he appeared in her peripheral vision, standing at the window that looked out on the dark woods beyond the cabin.

"Complications," he said softly. "I don't suppose I need any of those myself."

"So we're agreed?" She made herself turn to look at him.

He leaned against the window frame and looked back at her. "Yeah. We're agreed."

"If you'd rather we work separately from here on—"

"I'll try to control myself." His mouth quirked. "If you think you can."

"Somehow I'll soldier through," she answered, keeping her tone light.

He grinned at her effort at humor.

She felt as if her legs were going to quiver out

from under her, so she returned to the sofa and sat at the far end. "So, between what you learned about Blake Culpepper and what Briar told us about my parents' accident, which lead should we follow?"

"Both, I think," he said after a brief pause. He walked back to the sofa and sat on the opposite end, leaving room between them. "I'll put some feelers out to see if anyone around Bitterwood has spotted Blake Culpepper. See if I can get my hands on a recent picture we can show around."

"Does he have any outstanding warrants?"

"Not that I know of. I'll check into that when I get into the office tomorrow, too."

"And meanwhile, we'll take a look at the files on my parents' accident?"

"Absolutely. If you want to meet me at the office first thing tomorrow morning, we can take a look. I'll be in by eight at the latest."

"I'll be there."

Silence fell between them, tense with what they were leaving unspoken. Finally, Nix rose to his feet and pulled out his truck keys. "Thanks for dinner."

"You're welcome." Politeness, if nothing else, demanded that she stand up and see him out. She tried to keep a careful distance, but the cabin wasn't large enough for her to get so far away that she couldn't feel the tangible tug of his masculine appeal. It flooded her with instant heat.

He opened the door and stepped out onto the porch, turning before she could close the door behind him. He gazed through the open door, his expression suddenly serious. "I know you think you should have been able to protect your brothers. Both of them. I'm an older sibling, too. I get it. But it's not all on you. Maybe you should cut yourself a break."

Then he turned and disappeared into the darkness, leaving her staring out the door in confusion. Despite the chill of the night air flowing through the open door, she remained where she was until Nix's truck roared to life and the lights of the headlamps cut a slice out of the darkness as he drove way.

How could he know she felt responsible? She hadn't said anything of the sort when she'd told him about David's death.

But it was true, wasn't it? She felt responsible for his death, felt as if there should have been some way she could have foreseen the outcome of his dangerous trip and done something to stop him. He would have listened to her, wouldn't he? If she'd begged him not to go?

But she'd tamped down her worries and given him her support. She'd even driven him to the airport and given him a hug and a kiss goodbye, her blessing for his choices.

It was the last time she'd seen him alive.

She closed the front door and locked it, then walked in a fog back to the sofa. As she slumped onto the cushions and pressed her cheek against the back, she imagined she could still smell the clean, masculine scent of Nix's body in the nubby fabric.

Hell, she could smell him on her, not just in the weave of her cotton T-shirt but on her skin, as well.

She closed her eyes and breathed deeply, remembering the feel of his skin on her skin, his mouth on hers, the frantic thud of their heartbeats hammering chest to chest.

Complications, she thought, closing her eyes.

Easier to identify than to escape.

Nix ARRIVED AT the station earlier than usual, not because he was any more gung ho than the next cop, but because he hadn't seen the point of lying awake in bed, tormenting himself with all the things he'd wanted to do with Dana Massey, when he could distract himself with work.

Also, he knew if he got to work early, he could catch Briar Blackwood before she left the station at the end of her overnight shift in dispatch. He'd tried to reach Alexander Quinn to get a copy of the photo of Blake Culpepper, but the former CIA agent hadn't been in the office and nobody there could tell Nix where to reach him.

He caught Briar as she was gathering her things to leave. "Good morning, sunshine."

She cocked her head slightly. "Have you been awake all night?"

The girl with the X-ray vision, he thought. "A little insomnia. Thought I'd come in early to get a head start on the day. Listen, about your cousin Blake—"

She grimaced. "What about him?"

"Does anyone in your family have a recent photo of him?"

"Maybe his mama. You want me to ask?"

"Well, you might not want to mention it's the police who need it."

"If I tell his brother Randy I can probably get him to sneak it out of the house without her knowing. He hates Blake. Always thought their mama liked Blake best, which is kind of true, so I don't exactly blame Randy for it. Although Randy's not easy to like himself, come to think of it. But he'll get you the picture if I ask him to."

"That would be great," Nix said, unable to stifle a grin at Briar's candid appraisal of her family's foibles. It was one of the things he'd always liked about her—she didn't hold back what she thought, good or bad.

"Yeah," Briar said with a sigh, noticing his amusement. "We're a fine bunch, aren't we?"

"You are, for sure. Fine as they come." He touched her cheek with the back of his knuckles. "How you standing on money? Everything still okay?"

She stepped into the circle of his outstretched arm, letting him give her a brotherly hug. "We're okay. Aunt Jenny refuses to consider taking any money to keep Logan at night—she says he mostly sleeps the whole time and he's an angel even when he's awake, which you and I know isn't true, but she seems to like having him around. And it sure helps me not to have to pay a babysitter."

"Anything need repairing around the house?"

She shot him a look. "Anything needs repairing around the house, I'll be able to fix sooner than you would, and you know it."

He couldn't argue. Briar was handier than about anyone he knew.

Leaving his arm draped around her, he walked with her out to the employee parking lot, where her old Jeep Wrangler was parked not far from his truck. "You know all you have to do is give me a call, right? I know you've got it under control and all, but things happen, and you don't have to go it alone."

"I know." Briar gave him a hug, an impulsive

gesture from a woman who was usually inclined to keep her distance from other people. Her late husband, Johnny, had never tried to temper her independent streak.

On the contrary, Nix thought. Johnny had liked not having to put himself out much to care for his wife's needs. It had left more time for him to indulge his own whims and desires without worrying about Briar.

Too bad those whims and desires had run him up against somebody with a hunting knife and a grudge.

Nix returned the hug, noticing the womanly curves beneath his arms and the sweet, clean smell tickling his nose and wondering, suddenly, why he felt nothing of the fire that swamped his blood when he looked at Dana Massey. Why not Briar? She was as pretty as the hills she loved, as sweet as wild honeysuckle and as tough and resourceful as any pioneer who'd ever trod these mountains.

But she's not Dana, his mind taunted him.

Oh, hell, he was in trouble.

Headlights swept across the parking lot, making him squint as he let Briar go and glanced at the newcomer. It was Dana Massey's Chevy, he realized. He glanced at his watch. Only seven-fifteen.

Maybe she'd had a sleepless night, too.

He said goodbye to Briar and watched her drive away, staying where he was until Dana had parked the Chevy and started walking toward him.

He met her near the door. "You're early."

"You, too." She nodded at the taillights of Briar's car, still visible in the early-morning gloom. "Briar?"

"Yeah."

"I guess that was a brotherly hug?" She closed her eyes as soon as the words left her mouth. "Oh, no, that sounded terrible. Forget I said it."

"Forgotten," he lied, stifling his pleasure at her flicker of jealousy as they entered the station through the back door.

"Thanks."

"The file clerk won't be in before eight," he warned as they walked down the long corridor to the front desk, where he waited for her to sign in and receive a visitor's badge from the desk sergeant.

"I'll mooch some coffee while we wait," she said, already moving ahead of him down the corridor.

"Briar's going to get us a photo of Blake Culpepper," he told her as they stopped in the break room for coffee.

"Do you really think he could be behind what happened to Doyle?"

"It's as likely as the Sutherlands and Hales being behind it," he reminded her, watching her produce a large plastic coffee mug from her purse and fill it with coffee.

She stirred in two sweeteners, no cream and took a long swig, grimacing. "This is really terrible coffee."

"Sorry, should have warned you." He'd already had his morning coffee at home.

She shrugged. "Never have been to a police station with coffee worth a damn." She nodded toward the exit. He walked with her to the small communal office the detectives on the force shared. Nix was the only detective in the office, though the new chief of detectives, Antoine Parsons, was somewhere in the building. He'd stuck his head in the office earlier, called Nix a suck-up, then wandered off to do whatever upper management did at seven in the morning.

Dana pulled up the rickety steel-and-vinyl chair that sat in front of Nix's work space and rested her elbows on the desk. "So, do you think waving around a photo of Blake Culpepper is going to get you anywhere? I mean, he has a lot of family around, doesn't he?"

"Well, loyalty's a fickle thing, sometimes," he said with a shrug. "Blake has both friends and enemies around these parts, some of both in his own family. The secret is finding one of the enemies before the friends start throwing around threats and scaring them off."

"Is the militia movement a big thing in this area?"

"Yes and no. There are militia groups, but not all of them are really dangerous. Some of them are just guys who take the Second Amendment seriously and meet together to target-shoot, do a few drills and complain about government over-reach, and they're not entirely wrong, sometimes. They're generally law-abiding and cause us no trouble."

"That's not the case with the Blue Ridge Infantry," she said.

"No, it's not. They've been trouble from the start."

"And you think they've extended their reach down into Tennessee?"

"I don't know if the Blue Ridge Infantry even exists in its original form anymore." Nix leaned back in his chair until it creaked. "From everything we've been able to learn about Wayne Cortland's organization, he pretty much co-opted the militia for his own purposes."

"Along with a couple of anarchist groups and God knows how many hillbilly drug dealers." Dana rested her chin in her hands and looked across the desk at him. "But how cohesive a group are they now, with Wayne Cortland dead and his son missing?"

"*If* he's missing." Nix thought about his meeting with Alexander Quinn the day before. Quinn had intimated that Merritt Cortland could still be alive, but Quinn always had an agenda. Even if he knew for a fact that Cortland was dead, he would lie about it if it suited his own interests.

The real question was, what did Alexander Quinn want from Nix? What was his skin in the game?

One of his fellow detectives, Delilah Brand, entered the office yawning, arching one dark eyebrow at the sight of Dana sitting in front of Nix's desk. "Morning," she said, making faces at Nix behind Dana's back.

"Delilah, have you and Dana met?"

"Briefly, at the engagement party," Delilah answered, smiling as Dana turned with a nod of greeting. "What's the latest on the chief?"

"I called him last night and he said the physical therapist gave him the go-ahead to leave on crutches. So he thinks the doctor will finally spring him this morning." Dana checked her watch. "Of course, if I know anything about hospitals, that means he'll get out sometime this afternoon."

"Sure glad Laney has to deal with him and not

me," Delilah murmured, then looked up at Dana, apology in her eyes. "Sorry."

"No need to apologize," Dana said with a grin. "I wouldn't want to have to deal with him, either."

"Anything new on the investigation?" Delilah directed the question to Nix. He didn't have to ask what investigation. Everyone in the office took the attempt on the chief's life personally.

"We're following a couple of different leads." He summarized where they'd gotten in the investigation. "Don't suppose you know anything about Blake Culpepper?"

"Just that he's trouble," Delilah answered. "I'm from Smoky Ridge, you see," she explained to Dana. "Smoky Ridge families and Cherokee Cove families don't mingle much. Hell, if we followed the example of our ancestors, Nix and I should be mortal enemies."

"Why's that?"

Nix shrugged. "Hell if we know. Some of these family feuds go so far back, nobody remembers why we hate each other."

Dana looked thoughtful, but she didn't comment.

About thirty minutes later, Nix called the file room to see if anyone had arrived. The clerk, Robby Alvarez, had just clocked in and told Nix to come on down, so Nix and Dana headed to the other side of the headquarters building, where the department kept its old files.

"Everything prior to 1980 is stored off-site," Nix told her as they entered the file room. "But the file on your parents' accident should be here."

Dana let out a low whistle as she looked around the relatively small room. It was set up like a library, with tall shelves of file boxes separated by narrow aisles. Being relatively new to the police department, Nix had rarely had occasion to venture into the file room. A good thing, too, since the cramped space made him feel enormous and clumsy.

"How are they filed? By year? Alphabetically?"

"Alphabetically," he answered. "So Massey should be somewhere in the middle of all this."

Dana went straight to the middle aisle and started scanning the labels on the file boxes. Nix started at the other end of the aisle. They found the *M*'s near the middle and started going through the boxes.

"Damn it," Dana said a few minutes later, slapping her hand against the side of the box she was looking through. "I just went from Martin to Masters without finding any files labeled *Massey*."

"That's not right," Nix said with a frown, looking over her shoulder at the open box.

She moved aside to let him take a look. He

went through the files slowly, in case a couple of folders had stuck together, but she was right. There was no file for the Massey accident. "I wonder if it was archived already."

"I thought you said everything from 1980 forward was here."

"I thought it was." He walked out to the clerk's desk, where Alvarez was typing on his computer. "Alvarez, if I were looking for a file on a fatal MVA from fifteen years ago, would I look here or in the off-site archives?"

Alvarez looked at him as if he were stupid. "Everything from 1980 forward is in there," he said, waving at the file room. "We won't move any more files out of there until we run out of room again. I figure that'll be in about four years, based on the current crime rate."

"Has anyone checked out any of the files recently?"

"Let me see." Alvarez tapped the keyboard rapidly. "Detective Brand has a couple of files out on meth dealers in the area, and Detective Calhoun is looking at complaints filed against militia groups."

"What about the chief?" Dana asked. "Has he pulled any files recently?"

"He asked about a file a few days ago, but he was going to come look for it the morning after his engagement party." Alvarez looked up at Nix suddenly. "He was interested in an old MVA, too." He glanced at Dana, saw her visitor badge and added, "'MVA' is 'motor vehicle accident,' ma'am."

"Thank you," Dana said, a smile playing at the corners of her mouth.

"Alvarez, this is the chief's sister, Dana Massey. Deputy U.S. marshal Massey."

Alvarez looked mortified. "Sorry, ma'am. Didn't mean to condescend."

"No offense taken," she assured him. "Is there any sort of file index that lists the files kept here or in the off-site archive?" she asked.

Damn, Nix should have thought of that. "You keep an index on this computer, don't you?"

"Yes, sir." Alvarez called up the database. "What names, exactly?"

"Calvin Massey and Tallie Massey."

Alvarez looked at her. "Kinfolk?"

"My parents," she answered bluntly.

Alvarez shot her a look of sympathy. "Oh. I'm sorry."

"Thank you." She nodded toward the computer monitor. "What else do you need?"

"The exact date."

Dana gave it to him, and Alvarez typed in the information. After about twenty seconds, he turned to look at them, his expression puzzled. "It's not here."

"Not there?"

Alvarez shook his head. "There's no sign of any file on an MVA with fatalities on that date."

Chapter Ten

Dana's gut coiled into a tight knot. "You're telling me that there's no record of my parents' deaths?"

"Not in these files."

"That's not possible." She looked at Nix. "There had to be some sort of record of their deaths. I had a death certificate and I think there was probably a letter from the police department, affirming that the death was an accident, or we wouldn't have been able to get the money from their insurance policies." She rubbed her temples, fighting off the first twinge of a tension headache. "How could there not be a file on the accident?"

"Are you sure it happened in the Bitterwood jurisdiction, ma'am?" Alvarez asked.

"Their car went off Purgatory Bridge."

Alvarez blew out a long breath. "Yeah, that's Bitterwood jurisdiction, all right." He turned back to the computer and typed in something else.

Dana peered over his shoulder and saw that he'd used a span of dates covering the day before and the day after the accident. "What are you doing?"

"I thought maybe someone had misspelled the names on input, or maybe it happened close to midnight and someone entered the wrong date, but I'm not coming up with any files on or around that date." He looked almost as aggrieved as she felt.

"Is that unusual?" Nix asked.

Alvarez shot a worried look at him. "Very unusual. You can say what you want about the previous chief, but he made sure the record-keeping around here was good. We don't throw away anything, even when we probably should."

Nix traded gazes with Dana. He looked as if he wanted to give her a hug, and at the moment, she didn't think she'd have protested if he'd tried. But he apparently took their pact to heart, for he kept his hands to himself and turned back to Alvarez. "Can you take a look and see if there's any chance of a computer glitch or database error? I'll check back later."

"Yes, sir."

"And check with the Ridge County Sheriff's Department. They might have records, if for some reason they also answered the call that night."

With a nod, Alvarez turned back to the computer, hammering the keys as if he took personal offense at the system's failure to produce what they had asked for.

Nix flattened his hand against Dana's back. "Come on." He gave a nod toward the door, urging her out. In the corridor, he lowered his voice. "If there's been a clerical error, Alvarez will find it."

"But you don't think it's a clerical error, do you?" she asked.

He must have realized he was still touching her back, for he pulled his hand away quickly, flexing his fingers at his side. "No, I don't."

"Then what do you think it is?"

"I'm not sure."

She grabbed his hand and gave it a sharp tug. His gaze met hers, blazing with heat. She took a step closer to him as if drawn by a magnet.

He pulled his hand away and stepped back, though he didn't drop his gaze. Tension crackled between them, but she made herself retreat, as if distance could snap the tug of attraction ensnaring them.

She took a shaky breath and tried to focus her thoughts. "We're talking about my parents' deaths, Nix. If you have a theory about why the file is missing, I damned well have a right to know."

"It's only a theory," he warned.

"Understood."

He nodded toward the end of the corridor and started walking, forcing her to catch up. His voice low, he said, "You know about the corruption in this department. It's why your brother is chief of police now."

"Of course. But that corruption is fairly recent, isn't it?"

"We're not sure how far back it goes," he admitted.

"But fifteen years?"

"It could. We don't know. There might still be officers on the force who are on the take. It's an ongoing investigation."

The image of Doyle, bleeding and injured in his wrecked truck on a dark mountain road, flashed through her head, making her feel sick. "What if Briar's friend was right? What if my parents' wreck wasn't an accident?"

With a soft exhalation, Nix stopped in the middle of the hallway and turned to face her. "Then it's possible someone covered up the evidence that would prove it was deliberate."

She'd half hoped he'd tell her she was being paranoid. But the look on his face was anything but skeptical. He didn't just believe the rumor might be true, she realized.

He believed it was likely.

Her knees suddenly felt like jelly. She stepped

backward until her spine flattened against the wall, letting it prop her up.

Nix took a couple of steps toward her, stopping just short of touching her. "You okay?"

"Yeah. I just—" She blew out a long breath. "It was hard enough knowing someone killed my brother David on purpose. But my parents, too? And almost Doyle, as well?"

"We don't know for sure—"

"You think it's true," she said. "I can tell you do."

He dropped his gaze. "You see too damned much."

She made herself stand up straight, relieved that the temporary trembling in her limbs had dissipated. "So how do we prove it?"

His gaze snapped up to meet hers. "Don't you think you're a little too emotionally involved in this investigation already?"

Part of her knew he was right, but she'd be damned if she'd back off and let someone else find out what had happened to her parents fifteen years ago. Their deaths had changed everything for her and her brothers. Everything. Maybe David wouldn't have gone to Sanselmo if her parents were still alive. Maybe they'd have talked him out of it the way she hadn't.

"You can't leave me out of this investigation now," she said.

He looked at her as if he was inclined to do exactly that. But as she steeled herself to argue, he finally shook his head. "I probably should, but you'd just go around me and make my job that much harder."

She managed a smile. "You're coming to know me so well."

"But the next step, I have to take alone." He gestured for her to continue walking with him.

"What step is that?"

"If there's anyone who'd remember that accident, it's the former chief. Before his retirement, he'd been approaching forty years on the force, first as a patrol officer, then up the ladder."

"Was he already the chief at the time of the accident?"

"I believe he might have been. Either way, he'll remember." He looked at her, a warning in his expression. "But he's not going to talk to the sister of his successor, so you'll have to sit this one out."

She hated to be left out of any facet of the investigation, but Nix was already accommodating her far more than most local cops would be willing to do. "Okay. I can find something to do with my time."

He gave her a suspicious look. "Such as?"

She just smiled.

"I can't come riding up on my Harley every day," he warned with a quirk of his eyebrows.

"You have me mixed up with a fairy-tale princess," she said. "I can slay my own dragons."

"Be careful," he warned as she detoured toward the exit. He followed her to the door. "Some of the dragons around here don't play fair."

She flashed him a grin. "Neither do I."

He was still watching from the doorway, his brow furrowed, as she drove away.

FORMER BITTERWOOD CHIEF of police Derek Albertson had resigned from the force to escape the shame of being fired, but after the last two men he'd installed as chief of detectives turned out to be criminals, his options had been limited. As far as Nix and the other detectives knew, the chief was innocent of corruption himself, but it was hard for the man to justify keeping his job as top cop when he'd failed to root out the corruption in his own inner circle.

Since his retirement, Albertson had kept mostly to himself, spending most of his time at his modest house on Pinedale Road, just north of Main Street. His wife had died of cancer a few years earlier, so when Nix arrived shortly before eleven that morning, only the chief and an aging bluetick hound greeted him when he knocked on the front door.

Albertson's eyes narrowed at the sight of him. "What do you want?"

"I'm looking into a cold case," Nix answered, not seeing any point in polite chitchat, since Albertson showed no signs of welcome. "An MVA from about fifteen years ago, involving a couple of tourists."

Albertson's eyes narrowed further. "Tourists?"

"Well, actually, the wife was a former Bitterwood native. Tallie Cumberland."

Albertson's eyes were slits. "What's this really about? Did Massey send you here?"

"Chief Massey doesn't know I'm investigating his parents' deaths."

"Why *are* you?"

Nix cleared his throat. "You've heard about the chief's accident?"

Albertson nodded. He stepped away from the door but left it open, which Nix read as a tacit invitation to enter.

Nix let the hound dog sniff his pants legs and, finally, the back of his hand. The hound seemed to approve, wandering off to the corner of the small living room, where he picked up a rawhide bone, settled on the floor and started gnawing.

Albertson had already dropped into a well-worn recliner that faced an ancient television. The picture was on—a judge show, Nix saw—but the volume was muted.

Nix sat on the lumpy sofa next to the recliner. "The chief's brakes were tampered with."

Albertson's gaze slid away from the muted television and met his. "Really."

"You don't sound surprised."

"Nothing surprises me anymore," Albertson muttered.

"Do you know anything about it?"

Albertson shot Nix a hard look. "Is this an official interrogation?"

"Should it be?"

Albertson laughed. "No. I may not be happy the town saw fit to replace me with an overgrown surfer boy, but I don't hold it against the kid."

"Good to hear." Nix leaned toward him. "Did you know the Cumberland family believes Tallie and her husband were murdered?"

Albertson snorted. "The Cumberlands ain't exactly the most reliable folks you'll come across in these parts. You'd be wise not to put too much stock in what they think."

"Normally, I might agree with you," Nix conceded. "But this morning, when I tried to take a look at the accident report in the department's files, it was missing."

Albertson gave him a considering look. "Maybe someone had checked it out. Maybe the new chief."

"I asked. He hadn't. And even stranger, the file isn't listed in the database."

Albertson shook his head. "That's not possible. We kept records of everything that happened on our watch, even if it was a false alarm. That accident happened in our jurisdiction. I remember it. It would be in the files."

"But it's not."

"Who tried to find it?"

"Alvarez."

Albertson frowned. "That system is his baby. If he didn't find it—"

"It's not there," Nix finished for him.

Albertson was silent for a long moment. Finally, he sighed. "Good God, how far back did it go?"

He knew something, Nix realized. "How far back did what go?"

"The corruption." Albertson had gone pale, looking every minute of his sixty-five years. "I thought it started and ended with that bastard Cortland, but if the file is missing—" He looked up at Nix. "What makes you think it wasn't an accident?"

"Besides instinct?"

Albertson's mouth quirked slightly at his answer. "Besides that."

"Shortly before his accident, Chief Massey was looking into his mother's history. Apparently

Tallie never told her children anything about her life here in Bitterwood."

"I can see why she wouldn't."

"Did you know that some folks in her family believe her story about the babies being switched?"

"Wishful thinking," Albertson said firmly.

"What if it wasn't, though?"

"You realize you're believing a grieving little girl's story about her dead baby over the word of—" Albertson stopped short, slanting a look at Nix.

"I know the parents of the other baby were Nina and Paul Hale."

Albertson frowned. "How do you know?"

"Nothing stays secret forever in these hills," he answered.

"The Hales are good folks. They're not the sort of people who steal other people's babies."

"And Tallie Cumberland was?"

Albertson shrugged. "She was young and heartbroken. She wasn't thinking straight."

Nina and Paul Hale would have been nearly as young as Tallie, Nix thought. And if they'd found their son dead in his bassinet, how much harder would it have been for them to accept the loss knowing that a poor, unmarried young woman had a healthy little boy just a couple of hospital rooms away?

Would *they* have been thinking straight?

"What are you planning to do?" Albertson asked.

"I need to know if there was any reason to suspect the Masseys' wreck wasn't an accident. That's what I was hoping I might find in the file. But it's not in the archives." He looked pointedly at Albertson as something the chief had said moments earlier flashed through his mind. "You were wondering how far back the corruption went. Why?"

Albertson released a long, gusty breath. "Because of who investigated the accident," he admitted.

"Who was it?" Nix asked, although he realized what the answer must be.

Albertson sighed. "It was Craig Bolen."

DANA'S CELL PHONE rang as she entered Ledbetter's Diner in search of an early lunch. When she saw it was Nix, she answered quickly. "What did you find out?"

"Guess who was the primary investigator on your parents' accident?"

She thought a second. "Craig Bolen?"

"How do you do that?"

Her stomach twisted in a knot. She found the nearest empty table, pulled out the chair facing the door and sat heavily. "I could tell from your tone that you'd found something important. And since Bolen is already in jail for corruption—"

"It figures his criminal tendencies might have been in play fifteen years ago," Nix finished for her. "Where are you?"

"About to have lunch at Ledbetter's. Want to join me?"

"I can't. I'm on the road."

"Are you going to the prison to see Bolen?"

"I'll go tomorrow," he said. "Not like he'll be going anywhere."

"Why not today?"

"Because I just got a call from Briar," he answered. "Someone broke into her house while she was at work."

"Is she okay?"

"She's mad as hell, but otherwise, yes."

Dana turned her head toward the window. Outside, the day was looking gloomy, dark clouds swallowing the sun. She sighed. "Do you think it's connected to our stopping to see her yesterday?"

"Cherokee Cove isn't the most crime-free area in town."

"What did they steal?"

Nix was silent a moment.

"Did they steal anything?" Dana prodded.

"She wasn't sure. But they made one hell of a mess."

Dana closed her eyes, feeling a little ill. "Because she let a Cumberland into her house?"

"We don't know that."

She had a feeling she did know. "What the hell is wrong with the people in this town?"

"The same thing that's wrong with people everywhere," Nix answered, sounding a little defensive.

"I know. I'm sorry. I just—I hate thinking that someone went after Briar because of me." She groaned. "Did they bust up all her Mason jars?" She didn't even want to picture what kind of mess that would have made.

"I'll help her clean up whatever happened," he said firmly.

"I'd offer to come help," she said, "but since I might have been the reason she was targeted in the first place…"

"Don't beat yourself up about it. We don't know that's the case, and even if it was, it's damned well not your fault," Nix said forcefully. "I'll call you after I check things out, okay? Why don't you go on back to your brother's place meanwhile? Don't you want to be there when he gets home?"

Safety in numbers, she thought. "Good idea," she answered. "Just call me as soon as you know what's going on at Briar's. Promise?"

"Promise." He said goodbye and hung up.

Dana swallowed a heartfelt profanity and

shoved her phone back in her pocket, turning away from the window to look for the waitress. She gave a start. A slim, silver-haired man stood in front of her table, smiling down at her with twinkling green eyes.

"Miss Massey, I believe?"

She nodded, cocking her head. "I don't believe we've met."

"May I?" He gestured toward the chair across from her.

She watched with narrowed eyes as he sat without waiting for her response. He crossed his legs and leaned back as if he owned the place, looking at her with a placid smile. He was handsome and well-groomed, probably in his late seventies, although he carried himself like a man decades younger.

And suddenly, she knew exactly who he was. "Pete Sutherland, I presume?"

His smile widened. "You're as astute as you look."

It wasn't hard to put the rest of the puzzle pieces together once he'd affirmed her guess. "T. J. Spencer spoke to you."

"Not directly. But it doesn't take long for word to move around a town this size." Pete Sutherland lifted his hand, and a moment later, the young waitress who'd been standing near the counter was at their table, smiling down at him.

"Hey, Mr. Pete. You want your usual?"

"I do indeed, Christie." He looked at Dana. "Miss Massey?"

She supposed it would be churlish to ask him to call her Deputy Marshal Massey. "A turkey sandwich and water," she said to Christie.

The waitress smiled and hurried off to get their order.

"If you want to know anything about me, my dear," Sutherland said, his expression still amiable, "you need only ask. How can I help you?"

She stared back at him, nonplussed. He had an open, friendly face and spoke in a voice that held no unkindness or condescension. His accent was broadly Southern, but without the raw, twangy edge that characterized the accents of most of the people she'd met so far in Bitterwood.

He wasn't what she'd expected, and she hated to be surprised.

He looked at his watch, an old-fashioned pocket watch tucked into the jacket of his pin-striped suit, she noted. "I am entirely at your disposal for the next thirty minutes, but after that, I'm afraid, I have an appointment I can't postpone. A shame, really, since I do so enjoy spending time with lovely young women. Happens so rarely these days, I'm afraid."

"Did you know my mother?" she asked before she lost her nerve.

The look he sent her way was full of kind pity. "Not beyond the unfortunate circumstances that brought her briefly into our lives years ago."

"When she claimed your grandson was really hers?"

"Precisely." There was no anger in his response, no enmity at all. Only a benign sort of sadness that tugged at the corners of his bright eyes.

No, Dana thought with sinking heart, Pete Sutherland was not what she'd expected at all.

Chapter Eleven

"He was completely friendly and charming." Dana looked almost disappointed, Nix thought. He supposed he could understand her frustration, at least; she'd thought she had a prime suspect in the brake-tampering case in the Sutherland family, only to find Pete Sutherland held no grudge.

"People around here love the old guy, and for a reason." Nix unlocked his front door and let her inside.

"I thought people around here didn't lock their doors," she murmured.

"I'm a cop. I know better." He closed the door behind him and helped her out of her jacket. "Remember, I just got back from a break-in."

"How bad was it?" Dana turned to look at him, worry crinkling her brow. "Is she freaked out?"

"It takes a hell of a lot to freak out Briar," he said with a smile. "She's mostly furious, since they didn't seem to take anything."

Dana frowned. "They just busted up the place for kicks?"

"I'm not sure it was quite that random," Nix admitted, hanging her jacket on the coat tree by the door and shrugging off his own.

"I know you said it probably had nothing to do with my going there yesterday, but…did it have anything to do with my going there yesterday?"

"I honestly don't know." He waved in the general direction of the sofa and headed into the kitchen. "Want something to drink? I don't have much in the way of alcohol here. My parents aren't drinkers, so I never picked up the habit."

"Same here, same reason." Her voice was closer than he expected; he turned and found she'd followed him into the kitchen and settled in one of the chairs at the small breakfast nook. "Wouldn't mind a sandwich, though. I was a little too thrown by meeting Pete Sutherland to actually eat much of my order at the diner, and I'm starving."

"I can do better than that. I have a couple of nice fat rainbow-trout fillets in the freezer. Caught last fall right out of Blackbow Creek."

"I'll pretend I know where that is," she said with a smile.

"Just over the hill from here," he told her. "I'll see what vegetables I can come up with."

"Mind if I use your bathroom?"

He nodded toward the narrow hallway off the kitchen. "First room on the right."

While she headed for the bathroom, he looked through his pantry to see what he had in the way of vegetables. He decided on a jar of green beans and a smaller jar of peaches that his mother had put away from her surplus last summer. He had some cream in the refrigerator that hadn't expired yet. Maybe he'd get all fancy and whip up a topping for the peaches himself.

He put the plastic bag of trout fillets in a bowl of hot water to start them thawing and turned his attention to the green beans, trying to remember how his mother cooked them. She usually started with sautéed onions, he remembered, so he pulled out a skillet and started the oil heating.

By the time the onions were beginning to grow translucent, he realized Dana still hadn't come back from the bathroom. Adding the green beans to the pan and lowering the burner flame, he headed into the back of the house. "Dana?"

The bathroom door was open, the light off. But the door to his study was open a few inches.

"Dana?"

"In here." Her voice came from the study.

He pushed the door open all the way and found her standing in the middle of the small room, making a slow 360-degree turn to take everything in. She paused when she caught sight of him, her eyes wide with surprise.

"I thought I smelled turpentine, so I followed my nose." She waved her hand around. "You painted these?"

He felt heat rise up his neck. "Yeah."

She turned back to the paintings that covered all four walls. There were more than two dozen canvases, hung wherever he'd been able to find an empty spot. "They're beautiful."

He tried to see them from her perspective, taking in the shadings and colors. Landscapes, for the most part, images of the ancient hills that lay all around them, silent and secretive. He'd painted them in full autumn splendor and bleak winter chill, bright with spring's promise and slumbering in the steamy luxuriance of thick summer foliage.

There were specific places, too, like the dilapidated remains of an old barn, the frothy fury of water slamming into rounded boulders at the base of Crybaby Falls, even the lacy ironwork of Purgatory Bridge framed against a perfect blue summer sky.

Dana touched the painting of Purgatory Bridge, her fingers moving slowly over the rough texture of the acrylic paints he'd used to capture the old truss bridge. "Why do you hide them in here?"

He hadn't consciously hidden the paintings,

he realized, though it must certainly appear that way. "I like to have them around me."

"Do you sell them?"

He shook his head, horrified by the thought. "And become one of those Smoky Mountain folk artists you find painting for hire in all the tourist traps? No, thank you. I can't paint on demand that way."

"These paintings are amazing." She turned to look at him, her green eyes shining with delight. An answering flood of pleasure filled his chest, warming him inside out, as she slowly closed the distance between them. "Will you let me buy one?"

He shook his head. "But I'll give you one. Which would you like?"

"You pick. I don't want to take one that you'd miss when I'm gone."

He felt that bubble of pleasure inside him burst. He kept letting himself forget that she'd be leaving, sooner rather than later.

"Take any one you want," he said.

She walked slowly around the room, studying each painting carefully as she went. He drank in the kaleidoscope of expressions playing over her face as she puzzled out the nuances of the images. She seemed to be listening to them, as if they spoke to her the same way they had spoken to him in his mind, long before he'd committed them to paint and canvas.

She stopped, finally, at one of the more understated paintings in the room, a dead Fraser fir standing in the middle of a copse of still-living evergreens, its spindly white limbs bare of foliage. "It looks like a skeleton," she said. "The other trees don't seem to notice it in their midst. But the tree knows it's different. Still, it stands there with a sort of sad dignity, like it refuses to bow to its death."

She understood exactly what he'd seen in the dead tree, he realized. "Blight has killed a lot of the trees, but they don't just crumble and fall down. They keep standing, and in a forest full of lush green trees, those skeletons are the ones you notice."

"Ghosts find a way to make themselves known," she murmured. He supposed she spoke from experience, given her own past. She turned to look at him, her expression serious. "Can you bear to part with this one?"

"It's yours."

She looked as if she wanted to cry, but she managed to stay dry-eyed as she turned back to the painting. "Have you given it a name?"

"No. You can name it if you want."

Her throat bobbed as she swallowed hard. "I'll give it some thought."

"I think the beans are probably burning by now, so I have to get back to the kitchen. But stay here as long as you like."

Fortunately, he got back to the pan of beans before they'd boiled off all the liquid. The fish fillets were thawed enough to pop them in the oven for a few minutes to cook, so he took care of that task quickly and turned his attention to making whipped cream.

Dana returned to the kitchen to find him grimacing over his less-than-successful culinary efforts. "What are you doing to that poor cream?"

"Trying to whip it."

"Your whisk skills are sadly lacking." She took the whisk from him and started beating the cream with lightning speed, slanting a sly look at him. "And here I thought you were good with your hands."

He looked at the stiffening peaks of cream forming in the bowl and thought of at least two responses he didn't dare utter before he finally gave up. Everything running through his mind at the moment would catapult them right into that dangerous territory they'd agreed to avoid the last time they were alone together off the clock.

"No comeback?" she murmured.

"I thought you didn't like playing with fire," he said.

She set down the bowl on the counter and

turned to face him, her mouth opening to reply. But the oven timer started to buzz, and she made a face. "Nice timing."

Indeed, he thought.

DINNER TURNED OUT better than Dana had expected, given how clumsy Nix had seemed in the kitchen. The trout was crisp on the outside, flaky on the inside, and the green beans were tender and full of flavor, thanks to the onions and a few dashes of seasoning. Finally, he'd heated peaches in the microwave and let the whipped cream melt over them for dessert.

"Those green beans and peaches were homegrown, weren't they?" Dana asked as she helped him load the dishes in the dishwasher, amused that in his otherwise rustic cabin, he'd seen a dishwasher as an appliance priority.

"Straight out of my mama's garden." He put detergent in the washer and closed the door, setting it to run.

"Do they have a big garden?" Dana followed him into the small living room and sat beside him on the sofa, not bothering to keep her distance.

Maybe she wasn't as afraid of playing with fire as she thought.

"They till the whole side yard. That gives them about four rows of plants each season." He propped his boots up on the scuffed coffee table, smiling at her as she followed suit, nudging his foot with hers. He nodded at her attire—trim-fitting wool-blend trousers, a pearl-gray blouse and sensible flat shoes. "Is this how you dress for work?"

"Unless I'm on a fugitive hunt. Then it's usually jeans and sneakers. The better to chase down the perps."

"Was it hard to get this much time off work?"

She grimaced. "They forced me to take the time, remember? I have a ton of leave piled up, and my boss told me if I didn't take it, he was going to recommend a psych eval. Needless to say, I took the time off." She sighed. "Good thing I did, huh?"

"Except the point of taking time off was to get away from the job." He waved his hand at her attire. "And here you are, working on your vacation."

"My brother was nearly murdered."

"I know." He nudged her lightly with his shoulder. "But why do I get the feeling that even if nothing had happened to your brother, you'd still have figured out a way to get in on an investigation?"

"I like my work." She sounded defensive, she thought. He'd touched a sore spot.

"Do you like it? Or do you like to lose yourself in it?"

"There's a difference?"

"I think there is."

She frowned, giving the idea serious thought. "I'm good at what I do. I know who I am when I'm on the job. What's expected of me."

"And when you're not on the job?"

She leaned her head back against the sofa cushion and stared up at the ceiling, part of her wanting desperately to change the subject and the other part of her swamped with the need to tell Nix the awful truth about herself.

She took a deep breath and made the plunge. "When my parents died, I became the head of the family. I was the oldest. I was nearly out of college and about to start my life. So I became the decision-maker."

"And?"

"And Doyle practically ran away from home as fast as he could. He decided he wanted to be a casino security guard *and* a high roller. He was pretty good at the former and terrible at the latter, blowing about half his college money in one sitting before he wised up." She shook her head. "I thought that job was a terrible idea and told him so. I threatened to find a way to cut him off from what our parents had left us if he did something so stupid, but he just cut himself off from me and David and did what he wanted."

"But you were proved right."

"Not before I damned near split the family apart."

"Sounds more like Doyle's the one who did the splitting," Nix said.

He was being entirely too kind, she thought. "I shouldn't have forced him to dig in his heels and do the exact wrong thing. My parents would have handled it better."

"I don't know. I get the feeling your brother is pretty hard to handle in any circumstances."

"I thought I'd be glad when he had to come back with his tail tucked between his legs," she admitted. "I was going to tell him I told him so. But he only came back because of David's death."

Nix twined his fingers through hers, giving her hand a squeeze.

She wanted to pull away, to close up and protect herself from the rest of the story. But she'd already started this process of self-exposure. It was only fair to finish it, to tell him the rest.

"David came to me before the trip, looking for my advice. He knew it was a dangerous area. He knew I'd be worried about him, but he felt this profound urge to go. The poor farmers and laborers in Sanselmo had been political pawns for so many years. Manipulated by autocrats, then exploited by rebels. They just wanted food on the table and roofs over their heads. They didn't know about things like Marxism and fascism and democracy. Those were just words to them. David wanted to help them learn ways to provide for themselves whatever finally happened to their country. He just wanted to make a difference."

"Did you try to stop him, too?" Nix asked quietly.

She looked at him, feeling as if she were bleeding from the inside out. "No. I told him I couldn't make that choice for him. I still remembered the mistake I made with Doyle, see? I'd driven him to the wrong choice by being so inflexible. I didn't want to make the same mistake with David."

She saw the exact moment when Nix realized what she'd done. She saw the horror dawn in his dark eyes, saw the crease of his forehead and the sudden paleness creeping beneath his olive skin. "Dana, no."

"I sent him off to die."

Nix shook his head sharply, reaching for her. She resisted at first, loath to take his comfort when she didn't deserve it, but his determination overwhelmed her. He crushed her close, his mouth warm against her temple as he whispered in her ear, "You didn't kill your brother."

"Close enough."

He caught her face between his large hands,

making her look up at him. "You couldn't live his life for him. For either of them. All you could do, all anyone could have done, was love them and welcome them home once they found their way back."

She tugged at his hands, trying to pull them free from her face. "What home? After my parents died, everything fell apart. I don't have a home anymore. There's an apartment I go to every night, but there's no home there. There's no home anywhere." She blinked hard, trying not to let her tears fall. "Maybe—maybe if David had lived, it would have been different. But he didn't come home. He found his way back in a box."

"That's not your fault!" He covered her mouth with his as she tried to protest, dragging her closer until she felt as if she would combust from the heat that filled the narrowing space between their bodies.

Her resistance fluttered feebly against the rising tide of desire until it sank beneath the flood and died away. Nix's mouth softened over hers, coaxed instead of demanded, and she stopped fighting.

Maybe this was wrong. Maybe she'd regret it later.

That was nothing new, was it?

Nix's mouth slid away from hers, kissing a

tingling path across her jaw until his lips tickled her ear. "You're analyzing, aren't you?"

She curled her fingers through the crisp hair at the base of his skull, liking the rough texture against her skin. "Actually, I was trying not to think at all."

"Good."

Except now that he'd brought the subject up, she could no longer turn off her mind, she realized with an inward groan.

She sighed, pulling away from him a few inches. "*Is* it good?"

"Thinking keeps us from doing things like this." He let one hand play lightly over the bare skin peeking over the first button of her blouse, popping the top button open to reveal the lacy top of her bra. "Or this." He opened another button and brushed his fingertip over the swell of her breast.

She couldn't stop her back from arching into his touch. "Nix, as good as that feels—and it feels really, really good—we did agree not to do this."

"Agreements can be amended." He kissed the side of her neck, sending sparks dancing through her nervous system.

"On the fly?"

"Excellent idea," he murmured, catching her hand and lowering it to his lap, where she quickly discovered just how far gone the situation had gotten. She closed her eyes, fighting the urge to let her fingers stoke the fire between them even hotter. What could it really hurt? In a few more days, she'd be back home in Atlanta, Bitterwood nothing more than a memory, an interlude out of time she could remember without regret.

But it was that reckless thought, that tempting lie, that made the decision for her.

She pulled free of his grasp and stood with her back to him as she rebuttoned her blouse and scraped her hair away from her flushed face.

If she gave in, if she let Nix take her to his bed and finish what they'd recklessly started, would she be able to look back on this time in Bitterwood as a happy memory? Could she walk away from Nix with no regrets?

She was afraid she couldn't. Maybe she was already in too deep, feeling too much to make it easy to go back to her old life without wondering if she'd left something irreplaceable behind.

But she had a hell of a lot better chance of escaping this place unscathed if she didn't surrender herself completely, didn't she?

"I need to go home," she said, ridiculously pleased that her voice managed to emerge without a tremor. "Doyle's probably there by now. I should help Laney make sure he's settled in."

"I'm not sure the lovebirds really need you for that," Nix drawled.

She turned to face him. Whatever he saw in her eyes erased the slight smirk from his face. He stared back at her, taking a long, deep breath.

"Okay," he said. "You win. The agreement stands." He waved at the door, sinking back to the sofa.

"I'm sorry."

He shook his head. "You're probably right. Our first choice was probably the smart one."

"You'll let me know what you learn from Craig Bolen?"

He nodded, still not looking up at her. "What are your plans for tomorrow?"

"I thought I'd see if I can talk to the Hales."

His gaze snapped up. "I thought you decided that angle was a wild-goose chase."

"I don't think Pete Sutherland had anything to do with what happened to my parents," she corrected. "But that doesn't mean the Hales didn't."

He looked skeptical. "Good luck trying to track them down. I'm not sure they're going to be as willing to talk to you as Pete."

Maybe not, she thought as she grabbed her jacket from the coat tree and shrugged it on. But one way or the other, she was going to find out the whole truth about what had happened at Maryville Mercy Hospital three decades ago.

Chapter Twelve

"What do you mean, he's not available?" Nix stared across the desk at the state-prison warden, who gazed back with slightly narrowed eyes. "You were supposed to inform us of any changes in incarceration because of Bolen's possible connection to ongoing cases our department is investigating."

"He hasn't been transferred to another facility." The warden, a hard-voiced man named Joe Larrimore, spoke in clipped tones that reminded Nix of one of his old drill sergeants back at Parris Island. "He's in the hospital in Johnson City," he explained, referring to a larger town a few miles west of the state-prison facility.

Nix sat back, surprised. "Did he fall ill?"

The corner of Larrimore's mouth twitched slightly, but there was no humor in his gray eyes. "He fell, all right. Several times, apparently. Somebody beat the hell out of him in the showers yesterday."

An alarm went off in the back of Nix's brain. "Yesterday?"

"He was fine when he went into the showers. He didn't come back out. A guard found him a few minutes later."

"Do you know who did it?"

"We have our suspicions, but nobody's talking."

"What hospital?" Nix asked, rising to his feet.

"The big medical center, but you're not going to be able to talk to him."

"Why not?" Nix asked, turning back toward the desk.

"He's in a coma. Got a brain bleed. Doctors can't say whether or not he's going to come out of it."

The warning bell clanging in his brain went to full five-alarm status. "Has he had any visitors in the past couple of days?"

"No. We checked."

"What about your prime suspects? Have any of them had any visitors?"

Larrimore looked taken aback, as if the question hadn't occurred to him. "We haven't checked. We didn't figure Bolen got beat up on command. He's an ex-cop and he doesn't play well with the other prisoners. That's usually reason enough."

It was possibly reason enough now, Nix had to admit, but the timing of the attack on Bolen was curious. The morning before, he'd gone to old Chief Albertson and extracted the fact that Craig Bolen had investigated the car accident that killed Tallie Cumberland and her husband, and within a few hours, Bolen was brutally assaulted and nearly killed in prison?

"How long do you think it would take to check the visitors' log from yesterday?"

"Not long. We should probably check incoming and outgoing phone logs, too," Larrimore suggested. "Do you want to wait for it or should I give you a call later when I know more?"

"Give me a call," Nix decided, heading for the door. "I need to check on things from another angle."

On his way out to the parking lot, he dialed the phone number of the former chief of police. The phone rang six times with no answer.

He considered calling in a welfare check on Albertson, but if he guessed wrong, he might piss off the man so much that he'd refuse to help with any other inquiries Nix might have into the old cases he was trying to unravel.

He could be back in Bitterwood in three hours if he stepped on it. He'd keep calling Albertson on the way, and if he still hadn't gotten him, he'd stop by to check.

He thought about calling Dana to see what angle of the investigation she was planning to tackle that morning, but the way they'd ended their evening the night before seemed to shackle him from making any overtures in her direction, even with a good, work-related excuse for calling. She'd been pretty clear about putting herself off-limits to him on any personal level. And if he thought it was only because she didn't find him attractive, he might have been less frustrated by the thought of putting on the brakes.

But she wasn't immune to him. She felt the fire between them just as much as he did. He'd seen it in those smoldering green eyes, felt it in her trembling fingers and quickened breath.

She simply had no intention of seeing where that attraction could take them, and he had to respect her decision, whether he liked it or not.

Hell, she was probably the smart one between them. She wasn't going to be in Bitterwood forever. Her vacation days would run out, sooner or later, and she'd be hauling her pretty little self back to Atlanta again.

And where would that leave him?

Stuck in Bitterwood, wanting something he couldn't have.

THE SMALL JAPANESE restaurant in Barrowville came as a surprise to Dana, who hadn't expected to see a real sushi bar and hibachi in Ridge County's small county seat. Laney was waiting at a table near the back, waving her over as soon as she spotted her.

"Sorry I'm late!" Dana sank into the chair across from Laney with a sigh. "I've spent the morning trying to track down two of Bitterwood's best-known citizens, which you'd think wouldn't be that big a challenge. But the Hales are apparently not answering phones or voice mails, and their secretaries are downright snippy."

"You mean Paul and Nina Hale?" Laney asked.

"Yeah." Dana hadn't yet told her brother the latest about her investigation, so Laney probably didn't have a clue what she was talking about. "I've come across some information about my mother's life here in Bitterwood thirty years ago."

"Yeah, Doyle said he was having trouble getting a straight story when he started asking around. He hasn't been at it long, though. He's had a lot to deal with these past few months at the police station."

"I've gotten a lot more information since Doyle and I last talked about it. I haven't caught him up. He may think he's ready to hit the ground running now that he's out of the hospital, but you and I both know it won't be that easy. Broken legs have their own timetable."

"Tell me about it! He wanted to work last night and probably would have if I hadn't insisted he go to bed." Laney had stayed at Doyle's place the night before after bringing him home from the hospital. They'd assured Dana she was welcome to keep staying there, too, but she'd packed her things and gotten another motel room in Purgatory last night.

Dana grinned. "I hope you have better luck dealing with Doyle than I've had with the Hales."

"Why do you want to talk to them?"

"How much do you know about my mother's history here in Bitterwood?" Dana asked.

Laney shrugged. "Not a lot. I keep meaning to ask my mom what she knows about her, but I've been going crazy trying to get all the wedding arrangements finalized. I know we're keeping it simple, but Doyle won't even consider waiting past June, and while I'd have been happy just eloping to Gatlinburg, my mother nearly started crying when I suggested I didn't really want a formal wedding ceremony." She sighed. "I had to compromise, but it's about to drive me crazy!"

"I wish I were going to be sticking around here a little longer so I could help with the wedding," Dana said with regret. "Not that I have any experience with them."

"You will be back in June, though, right?"

"Of course!"

Laney looked relieved. "I'm not going to make you wear some horrible dress for the wedding, so you can relax about that. I'll give you a selection of dress styles I've chosen—the bridesmaids get to pick the style they find most flattering, and all they have to do is match the color. You can even get your fitting in Atlanta. And I'm paying for the dresses. My mother apparently put away a chunk of change toward my wedding fund I didn't even know about, and she's insisting I use it."

Dana thought about her own mother and felt a hard, fast rush of lingering grief. "Do whatever your mother wants, as long as it's not too crazy."

Laney's frazzled expression melted into sympathy. She reached across the table and squeezed Dana's hand. "I will. I know I'm lucky to still have her around. I just wish Dad were still here to see me walk down the aisle."

"Who's going to give you away?"

"Dave Adderly, believe it or not."

It took Dana a second to place the name. She looked at Laney, surprised. "He's the man whose daughter was murdered a few months ago, right? And you and Doyle rescued the other daughter—"

"Right. Doyle and I have become friends with the Adderlys since the murder and the kidnapping. It was Doyle's idea to ask him. Dave was really touched. I hope I can make it down the aisle without crying. He and Margo have been so amazing through this whole thing. They've had to deal with their grief over Missy's death, and now they're still dealing with Joy's lingering issues from the kidnapping. And you know they must feel so betrayed that Craig Bolen was part of the whole ordeal."

"Bolen was a family friend, right?"

Laney nodded. "I still can't believe he was involved with the kidnapping. You think you know someone…"

Dana thought about her own mother, about her own perceptions of who Tallie Massey had been. Could she reconcile the strong, loving, centered woman she'd known all her life with the scared, grieving girl who'd recklessly stolen another family's child?

"I was trying to talk to the Hales," she told Laney, "because I found out that when our mother was a teenager, she had a baby. The baby died in his bassinet in the hospital. And apparently, crazy with grief at the loss of her child, my mother tried to steal another couple's newborn right there in the hospital. That couple was Nina and Paul Hale."

Laney's eyes widened. "Oh, my God. Your mother tried to take Dalton?"

"Dalton?"

"Their son. They have only the one child, Dalton. He works with me at the prosecutor's office. In fact—" Laney turned in her chair and started looking around the restaurant. "There he is. I thought I spotted him when we entered." She nodded toward the corner, where a couple of men were ordering lunch. "Want to meet him?"

Dana couldn't see much of the man who had his back to them, but the other one, the one she assumed was Dalton Hale, looked pleasant enough. Short black hair, tanned skin, the glow of health and prosperity. He was a little on the plump side, with a ready smile he flashed at something his lunch companion was saying.

"He looks nice," Dana commented.

Laney arched an eyebrow. "You can tell that from his back?"

"Oh, I thought—"

Just then, the plump man spotted Laney looking at their table and smiled, giving a wave. The other man—Dalton—turned to see who'd drawn his tablemate's attention. He flashed Laney a quick smile and nodded in greeting before turning around again.

But that one brief glimpse of Dalton Hale was enough to send a shiver rattling down Dana's spine. Because the man who'd just turned around to face them looked like an older version of her brother David.

And David had looked just like their mother.

NIX PARKED THE department-issued Ford Taurus in Derek Albertson's driveway, noting the chief's car hadn't moved from its haphazardly angled position in the carport. There was no sign of trouble visible from the outside, but something wasn't right. Nix felt it like a prickle on the back of his neck.

He reached under his jacket for his Colt 1911. Quietly ascending the porch steps, he paused for a moment to listen.

No sound came from inside the house. No television, no radio, no voices raised in anger or hushed in secrecy.

Maybe Albertson had gone somewhere with a friend. It would explain why he wasn't answering his phone. Most people used cell phones more than home phones these days, but Nix didn't have the former chief's cell number.

Still, he couldn't get past the timing of Craig Bolen's beating. Just a few short hours after Nix had gotten Bolen's name out of Derek Albertson, Bolen had ended up in a Johnson City hospital in a coma.

What were the odds those events weren't connected?

Edging to one side, so that he wasn't standing directly in front of the door, he gave a couple of sharp raps on the wood.

He heard no movement from inside.

"Albertson? It's Walker Nix."

He waited through another long silence and

was about to head back to his car when he heard a soft shuffling sound from within.

"Chief?" Nix called again.

He heard a faint but distinct profanity from the other side of the door. With a scraping slide of the dead bolt and a rattle of the doorknob, the front door opened a few inches and Derek Albertson's face appeared in the narrow opening.

Nix sucked in a quick breath at the bruises and scrapes that marred the older man's face. One eye was swollen nearly shut and his lip was split in two places. "Who the hell did that to you?"

Albertson's answer was to step aside and let Nix in. He locked the door behind him and limped back to his recliner, easing himself down with an audible groan.

"Did you report this?" Nix asked when it became clear Albertson didn't plan to say anything.

Albertson shook his head. When he spoke, his voice was thick and hard to hear, as if he were speaking around a mouthful of pebbles. "I fell down. Clumsy me."

Nix looked at Albertson through narrowed eyes. "That's bull and you know it."

Albertson shrugged, wincing at the movement. "Maybe I should get me one of those alarm things you wear around your neck on a chain. You know, when you've fallen and can't get yourself up."

"Who did this to you, Chief?"

"Stop callin' me that," Albertson growled. "I ain't the chief anymore. Ain't ever gonna be again."

Nix swallowed a growl of frustration. "Did they threaten to come back if you talked?"

"You want something to drink? I could probably rustle up a beer. Oh, wait, you're on the clock. I might have some Coke in the fridge." Albertson made a show of trying to get up, but he dropped heavily into his chair before he'd managed to lever himself up even a few inches. "Help yourself."

"Craig Bolen is in a coma."

Albertson slanted a pained look at Nix but didn't speak.

"Doctors aren't sure he's going to ever come out of it."

Albertson looked away.

"Someone got to him in the showers at the prison." Nix crossed to stand directly in front of Albertson's chair. He leaned forward, putting his hands on the arms of the recliner so that his face was only a few inches from Albertson's battered mug. "Are you sure you just slipped and fell?"

"Positive," Albertson answered. His forehead was slick with sweat, and his one good eye was white-rimmed with fear, but he stood his ground.

"Okay." Nix straightened up and stepped back. Albertson released a long breath and looked down at his lap. "If you'd like to change your story, you know where to find me."

He made it as far as the door before Albertson spoke again. "When did Bolen get beat up?"

"Yesterday afternoon. A few hours after we talked." Nix turned back to look at Albertson. "When did you fall?"

"About an hour after you left," Albertson answered in a flat tone.

Nix realized it was as close to an admission as he was going to get. "Do you need a doctor?"

Albertson shook his head. "Ain't bled to death internally yet, so I reckon I'm gonna live."

"Are you sure?"

"Go on. Get out of here," Albertson said. "You ain't gonna find any answers here."

Nix pressed his lips to a thin line to keep from arguing. He'd known Albertson long enough to know the man wouldn't talk unless he was good and ready. Clearly, at the moment at least, he wasn't.

On his way out of the house, Nix took a long look around, wondering if there might have been any neighbors home to see who had visited the chief the day before, but there were only two houses in easy view of Albertson's house, and there were no cars or trucks parked in front of either of them. Still, Nix jotted down the addresses.

He could pull the phone numbers and give the neighbors a call later this evening.

As he got into the department-issued Ford, he took one last look back at Albertson's house. To his surprise, Albertson stood in the window, his battered face just visible between a part in the curtains. He looked back at Nix for a long moment, then stepped back, letting the curtains fall closed.

He looked terrified, Nix thought, and considering the beating he'd taken, who could blame him?

Until this moment, Nix had been convinced the attack on Doyle Massey was almost certainly the work of either Merritt Cortland or one of his lieutenants, seeking some old-fashioned hillbilly vengeance against the man who'd thwarted their plans for the Bitterwood P.D.

But now he thought Dana could very well be on the right track in pursuing the secrets of her mother's history. Craig Bolen could have earned a beating in the state prison because of his on-the-record statements about Merritt Cortland's criminal activities. Hell, he could even have been targeted for simply being an ex-cop—inmates liked to punish fellow prisoners who'd once worn a badge.

But whoever had beaten up Derek Albertson had done so for one reason only: to find out what answers he'd given Nix during their meeting the previous day. And Nix's questions hadn't been about Bolen or Cortland or the crimes they'd committed together. His questions had been about Cal and Tallie Massey's car accident fifteen years ago.

Whatever secrets Tallie had been keeping, she'd taken to the grave with her, and someone was willing to kill to make sure those secrets stayed buried.

Chapter Thirteen

Every nerve in Dana's body jangled as the two men at the corner table rose and moved toward them. The black-haired man gave Dana an unabashed once-over as they approached, but it was the taller man, the one with her brother David's green eyes, who stole her breath.

Was she seeing what she wanted to see? Was she so determined to keep her mother's memory intact that she was perceiving a family resemblance where one didn't exist?

Surely Doyle had met Dalton Hale by now, right? Doyle was chief of police in the county. Hale worked in the prosecutor's office. Wouldn't they have had reason to meet? And if Doyle had seen the same resemblance she now saw, he'd have said something.

She looked down at her tightly clenched hands and tried to regain her composure before the two men reached the table.

"Dana, this is Seton Flannery and Dalton Hale.

We all work together at the county prosecutor's office. Guys, this is Dana Massey, my fiancé's sister."

Dana made herself look up and smile, though she felt as if her face would shatter into tiny pieces from the effort.

Dalton Hale stood right next to her seat, his hand extended. "Nice to finally meet a Massey."

"You haven't met Doyle yet?" Hoping he wouldn't feel the tremble in her fingers, she shook his hand. He had a strong, firm grip. Clean, neat hands but not as soft as she might have expected for a man with a desk job.

"We've accused Laney of hiding him from us," the other man, Seton, added with a grin, offering his hand, as well. "We were supposed to meet him at the engagement party, but he went and broke his leg."

So Dalton Hale had been at the engagement party? Clearly she hadn't met him before she left with Nix.

She'd have remembered.

"We were beginning to think he was a figment of Laney's imagination," Dalton added with a lopsided grin so like David's that Dana had to blink back tears to keep them from spilling down her cheeks.

"I don't want to run him off now that he's popped the question!" Laney laughed and waved at the empty seats at their table. "Y'all want to join us?"

Please say no, Dana thought. *I'm not ready for this.*

"Sure!" Seton pulled out the seat closest to Dana and sat, turning to look at her. "So, if I'm remembering the scuttlebutt correctly, you're a deputy U.S. marshal?"

"Right." She forced a smile, trying to keep her gaze from wandering back to Dalton Hale's face. If she looked at him, she might lose what was left of her composure. "Are you a prosecutor?"

"Well, right now I'm a clerk," Seton admitted, some of his earlier confidence faltering a little. "But I'll pass my bar exam soon, and then I can start trying cases."

"A little cocky, there, aren't you, Seton?" Laney asked with a grin. "You don't even know who the D.A. is going to be after next year. We might all be out of a job."

"Oh, come on. We all know it's going to be our man Hale here." Seton grinned across the table at Dalton, and Dana couldn't keep her gaze from wandering across to the older man's face.

She tried to study his features without being obvious about it, not wanting to draw his attention away from his colleagues. His bone structure wasn't exactly like David's, she realized. He was wider at the forehead, with a stronger chin and jawline. But the sharp cheekbones were almost identical to David's. Her mother's cheekbones had been similarly prominent, and Dana herself had inherited that feature.

Dalton also had the same, slightly ruddy complexion as her own, also a gift from her mother. Doyle's skin was darker, like their father's, but David's had been slightly fairer, more prone to freckling like hers. Dalton's slightly wavy hair was the color of dark rust, a tone darker than Dana's and the same rich auburn-brown David had shared with their mother.

She had hoped taking a closer look at Dalton would drive out the thoughts racing through her head, but the more she studied him, the more of her mother she saw in his features.

Have I lost my mind? she wondered.

Or had her mother been telling the truth all those years ago?

"How long are you planning to be in town?"

It took a moment for Seton's question to pierce the confusion spreading like flak in Dana's brain. "I'm sorry, what?"

"How long are you in town?"

"Oh. Um, at least to the end of the week." Her vacation days wouldn't run out for another week past that, but she'd planned to spend part of the time back in Atlanta, taking care of some things she needed to do around the apartment, things that always seemed to slide to the back of the to-do list when she was working.

But with everything that had happened in the past couple of days, she wasn't sure she'd be ready to leave Bitterwood so soon.

"She'll be back for the wedding next month, for sure." Laney slanted a sly smile at Dana. Dana could see the matchmaking glint in the other woman's eyes and tried to send back a warning look without being too obvious about it.

She was not in the market for a relationship, in either the short or long term. And if she were…

"Do you like your work with the Marshals Service?" Dalton Hale's low voice, edged with a faint mountain twang, gave away his Smoky Mountain origins. Her mother's accent had been like that, she remembered, the roughest edges worn away by time away from the mountains but still possessing the light reminder of where she'd come from.

"It's never dull." She took the opportunity to give him another quick once-over. It was odd, she thought, how she was almost seeing him as David now. Or, at least, how David might look if he'd lived past his early twenties.

It was hard not to stare, hard not to feel an affection for him that should have belonged to her little brother. Dalton Hale was older than she was, but she felt a sudden, hard rush of protectiveness toward him that burned like fire in her belly. She wanted to know what his life had been like. Had he been happy? Had he gotten along with the people who raised him? Had they loved him the way he deserved?

Did he wish he had other brothers and sisters?

"Are you a Ridge County native?" she asked, though she already knew the answer. She knew where he'd been born and when. But maybe the question would lead him to more personal revelations.

Laney gave Dana an odd look across the table, her blue eyes sliding from her face to Dalton's and then back to hers. Suddenly, her gaze flicked back to Dalton's face and her mouth trembled open.

She sees it, Dana realized. *She can see that Dalton and I look remarkably alike.*

Laney's gaze slowly slid back to meet Dana's. Understanding gleamed in those eyes and Dana felt the sudden, disconcerting urge to cry.

She wasn't sure how she made it through lunch. By the time Dalton and Seton had to head back to the office, the strain of trying to act normal had given Dana a splitting headache.

Once the men had left the restaurant, she lowered her head and pressed her fingertips to her temples, completely at a loss as to how she should be feeling. Happy that she had another brother? Sad that she and the rest of the family had lost so many years with him? Enraged by what his family had taken away from her mother all those years ago when they'd stolen her baby from her and left their own dead child for her to mourn over?

"It's him, isn't it?" Laney said quietly. "Your mother's baby."

"He looks just like our brother David. And David always looked the most like Mom of the three of us."

"You and Dalton look a lot alike, too. Your mother was telling the truth." Though Laney's gaze was soft with sympathy, Dana also saw a darker emotion roiling behind her blue eyes. A realization, she supposed, of just how complicated life in Bitterwood was about to become.

She found her voice. "We can't know for sure without a DNA test."

"Maybe not, but I know what I saw. You saw it, too."

Dana reached across the table and closed her hand over Laney's arm. "You can't tell anyone."

"I wouldn't, but—what are you going to do about it?"

"I'm not sure," Dana admitted. So many years had passed, so much that couldn't be undone. Proving Dalton Hale was really Tallie Cumberland's son might be one hell of an uphill battle, especially if Dalton refused to cooperate. Maybe it would be better, since her mother was no longer alive, to let things lie.

Except someone had tried to kill her brother. And given the missing accident report, it was even possible someone had murdered her parents fifteen years ago. Had their deaths been engineered to cover up this very lie?

And if so, could she let her parents' murders go unpunished to prevent Dalton Hale from learning the truth?

Laney sat up a little straighter. "If any of this is true, and it comes out, what's that going to do to Dalton's bid for county prosecutor?"

It seemed a frivolous question to Dana, given all the other questions she'd just been pondering, but she supposed to Dalton Hale, the effect of a scandal on his ambitions would be a major consideration. Dana didn't suppose it would help him gain any votes, although these days, it was sometimes impossible to predict how a scandal would shake out. Dalton, after all, was an innocent in the mess. Even if it could be proved that his parents had stolen him from Dana's mother, no one could find him at fault.

Still, it would be easier to win an election as the son of a well-known and well-loved town scion than the son of the town pariah. People around here didn't care much for the Cumberlands. She'd seen that truth firsthand.

"I can't worry about what it does to his ambitions," she said finally. "Right now I'm trying to figure out if what happened to my parents fifteen years ago was really an accident or if it was murder."

Laney looked shocked. Dana supposed Doyle hadn't told her about their suspicions yet. "You think someone deliberately caused your parents' accident?"

Dana told her about the missing files. "It's pretty suspicious, don't you think, that those files are missing? And that Craig Bolen was the man in charge of the investigation?"

Laney scowled. "I'd believe Bolen capable of almost anything. But you're not saying he was behind the accident?"

"I don't know who actually made it happen," Dana said quietly. "But if they were killed because they came to town asking difficult questions about the Hale family…"

Laney's eyes widened. "You don't think the Hales were behind it!"

"They'd have the most obvious motive, if they stole him from my mother all those years ago."

"But they're good people," Laney protested. "They fund programs for the poor, give millions to charity—"

"And wealthy, charitable people never commit crimes?"

Laney sighed. "Of course they're as capable of crimes as anyone, but I know the Hales. And old Pete Sutherland is a complete sweetheart."

Dana thought about her own meeting with Pete Sutherland and couldn't disagree. "I met him yesterday."

"Pete?"

"Yeah. She told Laney about running into the man at the diner. "He's a real charmer. Maybe he doesn't know about Dalton's real parentage."

"Nobody knows about his parentage for sure." Laney lowered her voice. "Look, I think you're probably right. I mean, Dalton looks a lot like you, and you tell me he looks like David."

"You've never seen a picture of David?" Dana asked.

"The only picture of David your brother ever showed me is a candid shot of the two of them fishing in the Gulf of Mexico with your dad. The focus isn't the greatest. I couldn't really make out much about him."

Dana knew the picture. She'd taken it. The boat had been rocking like crazy on a windy day. She was lucky to have snapped a decent shot at all.

"I have a better one." She opened her purse and pulled out her wallet. She had David's senior photo from college. Sliding it from the photo sleeve, she handed it to Laney. "That's David about two years before he died."

After a quick look, Laney's gaze snapped up to meet Dana's. "I've seen college pictures of Dalton—he has some group shots on his wall at work. The resemblance is uncanny."

"I need to talk to Doyle."

Laney nodded. "Of course. He was still at home when I left for work this morning, but I wouldn't be surprised if he conned one of his cops into giving him a ride into the office."

Laney's instincts were dead-on; Doyle had gone into the office not long after Laney left. Since Laney had taken the afternoon off to deal with wedding plans, she went with Dana to the Bitterwood police station, intending to round up her stubborn fiancé and convince him to go back home to rest as his doctor had prescribed.

But Doyle wasn't alone in his office when they arrived. Walker Nix sat in one of the chairs across the desk from him. He stood as they entered, his gaze locking with Dana's.

"I thought we agreed you would wait until Monday to come back to work," Laney told Doyle, her tone more worried than scolding as she rounded the desk and bent to give him a kiss.

"I'm afraid that's my fault," Nix said. "I've come across a bit of a situation."

"So have we," Dana said bluntly, taking the chair next to Nix. "And it's a doozy."

"Bigger than the former chief of police having

the hell beaten out of him in order to find out why Nix went to visit him yesterday?" Doyle looked about as angry as Dana had ever seen her usually easygoing brother.

Dana looked at Nix. "How badly is he injured?"

"He'll live. But Craig Bolen may not."

"What happened to Bolen?" Laney asked.

In a couple of terse sentences, Nix told them about his visit to the state prison. "He's in a coma. His condition is critical."

"That's bad," Laney agreed. "But Dana's news is bigger."

"So spill," Doyle said impatiently.

Dana suddenly felt uncertain, now that she had to say the words out loud to her brother. "I think…" She paused, took a deep breath and started again. "I met Dalton Hale today. And I think he's our brother."

Both men stared at her as if she'd lost her mind.

Laney broke the ensuing silence. "I think she's right." She put her hands on Doyle's shoulders, dropping a quick kiss on the top of his head. "Call up the Ridge County District Attorney's office on the web."

Still looking wary, Doyle pulled his laptop closer and did as she asked. "Now what?"

"Click the button that says Meet the Staff."

Dana kept her eyes on her brother's face as he clicked the button, wondering if he'd see what she'd seen. If Doyle saw it, then she'd know she was right. That she wasn't just seeing what she wanted to see.

His brow furrowed, then rose. His gaze snapped up to meet Dana's. "My God."

"What is it?" Nix asked.

Doyle looked at Dana. "Show him that picture you keep in your wallet."

Dana still had the photo of David tucked just inside her purse. She pulled it out and handed it to Nix. He took a look at the photo, frowning. "Where did you get this?"

"Who does it look like?" she asked.

"It looks like..." He looked up suddenly, his eyes narrowing. "This isn't a photo of Dalton Hale, is it?"

"It's David," she said. "Our brother."

Nix's eyes darkened. "The resemblance is amazing."

"David looked the most like Mom," she told him. "Of the three of us, I mean. Even more than I do."

Nix ran his hand over his chin, his frown deepening. "As far back as that first night at the community center, at the party, some of the people around the room looked shocked to see you. Some even looked angry. Like you had no right to be there."

"Because I look like my mother."

"That's what I gathered."

"Who reacted that way?" Doyle asked.

"I don't remember exactly. But more than just one or two people."

"How could people not realize how much he looks like my mother?" Doyle asked. "I haven't had reason to meet him yet, but I would have known in a heartbeat."

"Maybe they *did* realize it," Laney said.

"And nobody said anything?" Dana shook her head. "My mother was run out of town because people believed she was a liar and a kidnapper."

"By the time Dalton would have been old enough for the resemblance to really come into play, your mother had been gone for years." Laney gently stroked Doyle's hair. "Maybe they thought there was no point in stirring things up after so long. As far as Dalton knows, the Hales are his parents."

"As far as we know, they are," Nix said.

Dana turned to look at him. "You just said—"

"I said he looks like your brother. And I'll admit, the evidence is stacking up in favor of his being your mother's child. But without DNA evidence, nobody's going to believe it based only on a photo and a lot of supposition."

"We need to get Dalton's DNA," Doyle said firmly.

"Good luck with that," Nix murmured.

"Nix is right," Dana admitted. "We're not in any position to demand a blood test from him. And do we have the right to throw his whole life up in the air just to prove our mother was telling the truth?"

Doyle released a long breath, looking at her with an old, familiar pain in his eyes. "So what do we do?"

"Whether or not Dalton is our brother doesn't matter at the moment," Dana said after a long pause. "Maybe, eventually, we'll try to find out for sure. But his parentage is a tangential question. The main one is, who tampered with your brakes the other night? And was there some sort of tampering that led to our parents' car crash fifteen years ago?"

"But what if those questions are related?" Doyle caught Laney's hands in his, and some of the stress faded from his face, as if her mere touch was enough to calm his troubled soul.

Dana felt a hard rush of envy. She was happy for Doyle, thrilled that he'd found someone who gave him comfort and support. God knew, he'd needed someone like that for a long, long time.

But his happiness served as a harsh reminder of her own loneliness. She'd always prided herself on being the kind of person who didn't need other people to be happy. But needing and wanting were very different things. She might not need to have the kind of relationship Doyle had found with Laney, but the more time she spent with the two of them together, the more she saw how they brought out the best in each other, the more she realized how unsatisfying her own life had become.

"Why don't we concentrate on one thing at a time?" Nix laid his hand briefly on her arm. The heat of his touch poured into her, spreading slowly through her limbs and into the center of her chest. When he dropped his hand away, she felt a twinge of regret.

"What do you have in mind?" Doyle asked.

"I don't think Derek Albertson is going to help us out," Nix said. "After the beating he took, I'm not sure I blame him."

"How did somebody know you'd talked to Albertson?" Dana asked, worried by the implications.

"I think maybe I'm being followed," Nix admitted. "I haven't exactly been looking for a tail, although you can bet I'll be doing so now."

"If Albertson won't help us, and Bolen can't, where do we look next?" she asked.

"Bolen may have been the lead detective on the accident investigation, but he wasn't the only person on the case," Nix answered. "If there's anyone in the world besides Derek Albertson who'd know who was doing what in this department fifteen years ago, it's Alvin Pitts. He retired from the police force a few years back." Nix pushed to his feet, pulled the jacket off the back of the chair where he'd draped it and shrugged it on. "I'm going to see what he remembers. And this time, I'm sure as hell not going to let anyone follow me."

Chapter Fourteen

"I've been wondering when someone was going to finally ask me about Tallie Cumberland's wreck." Alvin Pitts rose from a crouch over his bed of yellow crookneck squash and squinted against the bright afternoon sun. Nix had caught him in the middle of weeding the small vegetable garden growing beside his neat little bungalow on Old Purgatory Road.

Nix struggled to keep a rush of excitement in check. "Why's that?"

Pitts picked up the canvas bag he'd been using to discard the weeds and slung it over his shoulder, nodding for Nix to follow him to the front porch. He dropped the bag of weeds there and opened the screen door. "Have a seat. You want some iced tea? Martha's gone shopping with her sister, but she left a big pitcher in the fridge."

"Sure." Nix was relieved that Pitts's wife was out. He had a feeling Pitts might be more forthcoming without an audience.

Nix settled on one of the two faded cane rocking chairs that flanked the front door. The porch eaves tempered the afternoon warmth, aided by a light breeze from the west. Pitts's house was surrounded by the lush woods that lined Old Purgatory Road for miles, giving a sense of isolation even though the next house down the road was only a quarter mile away.

"The wreck happened a couple of miles down the road, you know." Alvin Pitts returned to the porch with a couple of glasses of sweet iced tea.

"I know." Nix took the glass Pitts offered. "Did you know the new chief had a wreck in almost the same place?"

Pitts nodded. "So I heard. You know he's Tallie's son, don't you?"

"I do. Her daughter's in town, too."

Pitts gave him an interested look. "I heard that, too. What's she like?"

Nix wondered how to answer that question without giving away too many of his own secrets. "She looks a bit like her mother, from all accounts. In her mid-thirties but looks about ten years younger when she smiles. She's a deputy U.S. marshal out of Atlanta."

Pitts sipped his tea and gave Nix a long, considering look. "She gettin' any guff around town?"

"Why would she?" Nix asked carefully.

"On account of lookin' like her mama." Pitts

set his glass on the flat arm of his rocking chair, holding it loosely to keep it from sliding off as he rocked slowly, each roll of the rockers making the porch floor creak. "You're from Cherokee Cove, Walker. I reckon you've heard all the stories by now."

"You sound as if you don't believe them."

Pitts laughed. "Never believe more than half the stories you hear around these parts. And even those you need to investigate closely."

"Were you involved in the investigation of the car crash that killed Tallie and her husband?"

The porch floor creaked a few more times before Pitts answered. "I was there that night. Helped winch them up out of the gorge."

"Did you know the files on that accident are missing from the file room at the station?"

Pitts shot Nix a quick, narrow-eyed look. "No, I didn't."

"There would have been files on the accident, wouldn't there?"

"Of course. I added some of the information myself."

"Did you ever go back and look at them?"

Pitts shook his head. "I did not."

"You sound as if you wish you had."

The older man released a long breath before he spoke again. "I wish I'd done a lot of things differently when I was on the force. But back then,

I tried to get along, not make too many waves. Benton was still alive then, and we were up to our eyeballs in hospital bills all the time. I couldn't afford to lose the job."

The wistful sound of Pitts's voice touched an answering chord in Nix's chest. Benton Pitts had been one of Nix's best friends in elementary school. A bright, active kid with sandy-blond hair, blue eyes and a face full of freckles, Benton had always been a daredevil, sometimes tempting Nix into the kind of trouble he remembered with a mixture of fondness and horror.

Five days after his thirteenth birthday, Benton, Nix and several of their schoolmates had gone swimming in Blackbow Creek in the middle of a long, hot July. Benton, always one to look for excitement, had coaxed several of the boys, including Nix, into diving into a deep part of the creek from Bald Rock, a big granite outcropping that rose nearly ten feet over the water.

Nix had gone first, landing belly-first and nearly sucking a gallon of creek water into his lungs as he fought to breathe again after the force of impact. Benton had gone next, entering the water with a clean, perfect swan dive.

But the bottom was closer than he'd expected. He'd hit creek bed, breaking his neck. Nix and the other boys had managed to keep him from drowning, but the damage to Benton's spine had been done. He'd been a quadriplegic for the rest of his life, dying too young at the age of twenty-five.

"I still miss Benton," he murmured, lifting his glass slightly in a toast.

"He was real proud you became a marine," Pitts said with a faint smile. "You know he always wanted to be one himself."

Nix squelched a hard rush of regret and got to the point of his visit. "Why do you reckon someone bothered to remove the files on Tallie Cumberland's car crash?"

Pitts gave him a considering look. "I'd say you must already have a pretty good idea why, or you wouldn't have come out here to see me."

"Was there any indication of tampering on the vehicle?"

Pitts looked out across the yard toward the woods. "There wasn't any fluid in the brakes when the mechanic examined it. He said it looked like the line was cut, although he said it could have happened when the car went off the bridge and down into the gorge."

Nix heard hesitation in his old friend's voice. "But?"

"But there was brake fluid on the road that night."

"On the road?"

Pitts nodded. "I collected it myself. Turned it over as evidence."

"And you're sure it was brake fluid?"

"I've been working on cars my whole life. I know brake fluid."

Anger hissed low in Nix's chest. "Which means the brake fluid was leaking out before they went over the bridge."

Pitts nodded. "That was my conclusion. Not that anybody wanted to hear it."

A woman and her husband had died, Nix thought, and people in the police department hadn't followed up on all the clues suggesting it was a homicide, not an accident? "Why would the cops ignore that evidence?"

Pitts didn't speak. But Nix could tell he knew the answer. His determination hardened. "Pitts, who wanted Tallie dead?"

Pitts took a long drink from his tea glass, as if needing time to organize what he was about to say. "If you'd like to know who in town would just as soon have never seen Tallie again, I can give you a few names. Startin' with old Pete Sutherland."

Nix shouldn't have been surprised, he supposed, considering what they'd learned about Tallie's time at Maryville Mercy Hospital and the allegations she'd made against Sutherland's daughter and son-in-law. But he couldn't reconcile the smiling man who'd been playing Santa at the community center for the past three decades with the sort of malignance that would rip a newborn baby from his mother.

"Don't let his smiles fool you," Pitts said quietly. "A man don't get where Pete Sutherland has in life without a ruthless streak."

"What about Paul Hale?" Nix asked.

"He's a possibility, too," Pitts conceded.

"Because Tallie tried to take his son?"

Pitts's sharp blue eyes met Nix's. "No. Because they took *her* son."

DANA SLUMPED IN the chair across from her brother's desk and stared at David's photo, her heart so tangled up with conflicting emotions she could barely breathe. He was almost twenty-two when he'd taken his senior photo, on the cusp of the exciting, meaningful life he'd been planning since he was sixteen.

Had he known it could end so soon? Or, like so many people his age, had he thought himself immortal?

"I miss him, too."

Dana looked up to find her brother's warm gaze watching her. "He was the best of us."

Doyle smiled sadly. "He was."

"Do you ever wonder what he'd be like now?"

"All the time."

She felt the hot sting of tears behind her eyes. She blinked hard to hold them back. "I have these dreams sometimes. Where I'm trying to talk him out of going to the jungle. And he just smiles at me and tells me we're already there. I look around, and there's nothing but jungles and rebels all around us. I wake up sweating and so full of guilt I can barely breathe."

"It's not your fault, Dana."

"He wanted my advice about going. I told him to follow his heart."

"I told him he was an idiot, putting his neck on the line for people who'd probably just hate him for it," Doyle said. "Want to take a bet as to which one of us really spurred him into going?"

She closed her eyes. "You're such an idiot, Doyle."

"I know."

"David did what he wanted," she said after a long, painful moment. "Nothing you or I said would have made any difference."

"I know. But it's taken me all these years to figure it out."

She opened her eyes to look at her brother. "You're really happy now, aren't you?"

"At the moment, not so much," he admitted with a grimace. "But overall, yeah. I am."

"Laney's wonderful."

He smiled. "She's way too good for me."

"Well, yeah, of course, but I wouldn't say that

aloud too often or she might believe it." Dana scrounged up a lopsided grin and shot it his way.

"I wish you weren't going back to Atlanta."

She felt a hard tug in the center of her chest. "I have a life there."

"You have an apartment and a job. That's not a life."

"I have friends."

"That you never talk about. Have you called anyone in Atlanta since you've been here?"

She shook her head. "I've been a little busy."

"All the more reason to call a friend for a little moral support."

"My work keeps me on the go all the time." Even to herself, the excuse sounded lame.

"You could ask for a transfer to the Knoxville office."

She cocked her head sideways, looking at him suspiciously. "Why do you care where I work? You've been fine with my being hundreds of miles away for a long time now."

"I haven't been fine with it," he admitted. "I've missed you like hell."

She stared at him. "You practically cut yourself off from me, Doyle. You went off and did your own thing and didn't seem to give a damn what I was up to."

He gave her a pained look. "I know. Like you said, I'm an idiot. But I did miss you. Every damned day. We're all we have left, and I guess maybe I was running hard from that thought, because you—" He stopped short, looking as if someone had gut-punched him. "I thought if I went my own way, made my life away from you—"

"Then if something happened to me, it wouldn't destroy you?"

He chewed his lower lip. "I'm sorry. I've been so selfish."

The tears she'd tried to stanch spilled down her cheeks. "I thought you blamed me for David's death."

He stared at her with horror. "My God. No. Never."

She pressed her hand over her mouth, fighting a sob.

Doyle levered himself to his feet, grabbing at the crutches leaning against the desk. He sent one flying and growled a profanity, dropping back in his seat.

Dana retrieved the crutch and set it against the desk, then crouched in front of her brother's desk chair. She cradled his face between her hands. "I love you. I don't tell you that nearly enough."

He tugged her into a fierce hug. "I love you, too. Always have, always will. No matter what."

She laid her head against her brother's heart, listening to the strong, steady beat, and felt as if a lifetime of poison was slowly seeping out of her body, leaving her feeling light and free. Even remembering why she was still here in town wasn't enough to break through that sudden sense of relief.

"What are we going to do if we prove that Dalton Hale is our brother?" She eased out of her brother's embrace and settled on the edge of his desk, looking down at him.

"I'm not sure," he admitted. "I guess it depends on whether or not we find out someone in his family is behind the attack on me."

"And what happened to Mom and Dad," she added soberly.

"We still don't have any proof it was anything but an accident."

She sighed. "No proof, but a lot of questions."

"Another good reason for you to stick around Tennessee for a while longer?" he said, his eyebrows rising.

She smiled. "We'll see."

His grin in response made him look fifteen again, still the smart aleck who took delight in turning her orderly life into chaos. *God,* she thought, *I've missed you, little brother.*

"YOU DON'T LOOK SURPRISED," Alvin Pitts observed. Nix met the older man's suspicious gaze.

"There have been some developments in the stolen-baby case."

"The case? What case? As far as anyone in this town is concerned, the stolen-baby case was closed over thirty years ago."

"Dana Massey met Dalton Hale today."

Pitts shot him a troubled look. "And?"

"Dana says Dalton Hale looks just like her younger brother. Who looked just like their mother. She showed me a photo of her younger brother. She's right. Hale looks just like him."

Pitts slumped lower in his rocker. After a long moment of silence, he asked, "Do you know how Tallie Cumberland was able to afford a bus ride out of town?"

"No," Nix answered. The question had never occurred to him.

"I gave her the money. And told her where to go. I have a cousin in south Alabama who runs a bait shop. Lester was always needin' good help, and I figured Tallie would fit the bill. Honest girl, hardworkin'. Not a bit like most of the rest of the family."

"So you gave her bus fare to Alabama."

"I'd check on her now and then, for several months. Ask Lester how she was doin' at the job. He liked her fine. Last time I spoke to him about her, years and years ago, he said she was seeing a nice young man. A state trooper."

Nix smiled faintly. "Cal Massey?"

Pitts nodded slowly. "Lester said he treated her real nice."

"You didn't keep up with her after that?"

Pitts shrugged. "She got a better job and left the bait shop. I didn't have any way of tracking her after that."

"What makes you think she was telling the truth about the baby?"

"Because Tallie Cumberland wasn't a liar. She might keep a secret or two—never did tell anyone who the baby's daddy was, as far as I know. But she didn't tell lies. The girl looked me in the face and told me the baby that died wasn't her baby. That she found her baby two doors down, in the room with Nina Hale. And God help me, I believed her."

"Why didn't you do anything to help her?"

"What could I have done?" Pitts asked. "I wasn't that much older than the girl myself. Fresh on the force, just tryin' to make a life for myself and Martha. Benton was on the way then—Martha had just found out."

Nix supposed he could understand a man not wanting to make waves when all he had was his belief in a teenage girl's word. "I guess everybody else believed the Hales."

"You guess right."

"I'm surprised Tallie gave up. From what I hear about her, she wasn't a quitter."

A weak smile creased Pitts's face. "She didn't give up for a long time. Drove folks around here crazy with it, if you want to know the truth."

"I thought she left town soon after the birth."

"Oh, no, son. It was nearly a year later before she went. By then, the Hales were talkin' restraining orders and defamation lawsuits." Pitts shook his head sadly. "They'd made life miserable for her folks and everybody who knew 'em. The folks in Cherokee Cove practically drove the Cumberlands out of town because of the feud between Tallie and the Hales. They were afraid the Hales and Sutherlands would call in loans and put pressure on their places of business if they didn't shun her and her family."

Which explained a lot, Nix realized, about the stories he'd heard about the Cumberlands his whole life.

"Is that what made Tallie give up finally and leave town?"

Pitts looked out across the woods, his gaze distant, as if he was watching the past play out in his mind. "She saw the boy with Nina Hale," he answered. "She ran across them at Little Creek Park in Edgewood. I reckon she'd gone there to try to talk to Nina alone, without Paul or old Pete there to run interference."

"She was stalking her?"

Pitts shrugged. "Some folks might call it that."

"Did she talk to her?"

Pitts shook his head. "She watched them a little while. Just watched Nina playing with that little boy. Tallie told me afterward it was like watching her heart rip to pieces and stitch itself back up, all at once."

Nix wasn't sure he understood. "All she did was watch?"

"I reckon it was all she had to do. I might have my suspicions about old Pete Sutherland, and I might agree Paul Hale has it in him to rip a baby out of his mama's arms for his own reasons, but I don't for a second believe Nina Hale knows that boy ain't her son. She's done nothin' but love him and take care of him like a mama bear since the day she left the hospital with him in her arms. I reckon watchin' her with that child a few minutes convinced Tallie of the same thing."

"So she decided not to take him away from the only mother he knew."

"She came to me cryin' like a baby. Told me she'd seen a different way to love her little boy."

A hard shudder of sympathy rocked through Nix, settling deep in his chest. "But she couldn't bear to stay around and see what she couldn't have?"

"Exactly." Pitts sighed. "So I helped her leave."

Nix rubbed his jaw, wondering if he would have had as much strength as that little mountain girl who'd chosen her son's happiness over her own. "Just one question, then. Why would anyone have wanted to hurt her and her husband fifteen years ago? She'd left town, stopped making a stink. What kind of threat would she have posed?"

"You don't know why she came back here to Bitterwood?"

Nix looked at the grizzled old former cop and realized the only possible answer. "Fifteen years ago, Dalton Hale had just turned twenty-one."

"He wasn't a kid anymore. He was old enough to hear the truth," Pitts said with a nod. "She and her husband came to talk to me. I reckon they might have talked to some other people, as well."

"They were going to tell Dalton the truth," Nix realized.

"I think that's exactly what they were going to do." Pitts met Nix's gaze, his expression grim. "And someone made damned sure they didn't get the chance."

Chapter Fifteen

Dana had never been any good at waiting for news. She preferred to take action, make things happen, rather than sit around and let things happen to her. Waiting for the phone to ring was a terrible way to spend her time, she decided, so she left her car at the police station and walked down Main Street toward the small business district to look for that engagement present for Doyle and Laney she'd never had the chance to purchase.

There weren't many shops in Bitterwood that sold anything appropriate as a gift for a pair of soon-to-be newlyweds, she quickly discovered. Why she hadn't taken full advantage of the shopping opportunities back in Atlanta, she didn't know.

Check that—she *did* know. She'd been working right up to the last minute, trying to come up with a reason to postpone her trip to Bitterwood and cancel her vacation days. Work had become the only thing that made any sense in her life in the past few years, maybe because anything approaching a personal relationship scared the hell out of her.

Look what she'd done here in Bitterwood. She'd met an attractive, interesting, intelligent man who clearly found her appealing, and she'd turned their relationship into work. Although, in her defense, it *was* a crime that had brought them together in the first place.

But nobody had forced her to use the attempt on her brother's life as a barrier between her and Nix. She'd come up with that excuse all by herself. She'd been the one to put on the brakes when things between them had started to heat up. Not Nix.

Over the past few years, she'd been doing a lot of hiding behind walls, hadn't she? Because of losing her parents and David? Because of a few less-than-happy endings in her own love life?

She'd never thought of herself as a coward, but she was beginning to wonder if it wasn't fear that ordered her life these days. Had she gained her reputation as a tough, hard-driving deputy U.S. marshal only because she'd rather take risks in her job than take any risks with her heart? Had she used her job as another wall to protect herself from what really scared her?

The trill of her cell phone felt like a giant reprieve from her uncomfortable bout of introspection. *Please be something I can do,* she thought as she looked at the unfamiliar phone number on her cell phone display. "Hello?"

"Good afternoon, Miss Massey."

It took a moment to place the cultured drawl. "Mr. Sutherland. How did you get my number?"

"I spent years as a newspaperman, my dear. I have my ways." His voice was tinged with amusement and a friendly sort of charm. "I've arranged for you to meet my daughter and her husband."

She blinked with surprise. "Really."

"I understand you were trying to reach them earlier today. As you can imagine, they were hesitant to readdress the unpleasantness of the past, but I assured them you were a reasonable and civil person. They have nothing to fear from you, do they?"

She supposed it depended on whether or not she came to believe they were complicit in the abduction of her half brother, the murders of her parents and the attempted murder of her brother. But she wasn't stupid enough to say so out loud. "Of course not. I'm just trying to fill in all the blanks my mother's death left for me. There was a lot about her past she never told us."

"Perhaps you should honor her wishes and let the past lie undisturbed," Pete said gently.

A part of her wished she could take his advice, even if she questioned his motives for offering it. If what she'd learned already meant what she thought it did, she had a lot of hard decisions to make.

But letting the past lie undisturbed wasn't something she could do, no matter what happened. Not if it meant turning a blind eye to murder.

"I can't do that," she said.

There was a long pause. "I had a feeling you'd say that." Pete sounded both resigned and a little regretful. "My daughter and her husband are understandably hesitant to meet you in a public venue. This is a small town and people talk."

A finger of unease traced a cold path up her spine. "Where do they want to meet?"

"They have a cabin on Copperhead Ridge. A small place they use in the summer. It's private and well away from curious eyes. I'm afraid you'll have to walk about a quarter mile past where vehicles can travel. Will that be a problem for you?"

"No," she said, even though she didn't like the sound of where the Hales wanted to meet her. Secluded and accessible on foot wasn't anywhere near an optimal choice. "I'll be bringing someone with me."

"I don't think Nina and Paul will agree to that."

What were they negotiating here, she wondered, an international treaty? "You can understand *my* hesitation."

"And surely you can understand theirs. This matter was closed decades ago, as far as my daughter and son-in-law are concerned. Meeting with you is a kindness on their part."

Unless she found evidence to force them to talk to her in an official capacity, Sutherland was right. If she wanted to speak with the Hales—and she most definitely did—she would have to deal on their terms.

But she'd still try to get Nix to be there, even if he stayed in her car. She didn't want to take any stupid chances if she didn't have to.

"What time?" she asked.

"They'll be at the cabin after four this afternoon. Can you be there?"

"I'll have to get directions."

"No directions necessary," he said with a hint of humor. "Bitterwood is not a large place, and you can almost certainly see Copperhead Ridge from where you're standing. You need only to follow Main Street until it becomes Edgewood Road. The Copperhead Trail marker is obvious. Turn left at the marker, park in the lot by the trailhead and follow the trail until you reach the first trail shelter. From there, you should see the path to the cabin on the right. Would you like me to have Nina or Paul meet you there?"

"That might be a good idea," she said. He spoke as if the directions he was giving her were simple enough for a child, but this might be her only chance to ask the Hales about what had happened at Maryville Mercy Hospital all those years ago. She didn't want to blow it by getting herself lost.

"I'll arrange it," he said. "I wish I could be there, but I have business to attend to."

"Thank you for arranging it, Mr. Sutherland. It's very kind of you." Assuming he had no ulterior motives, she added silently after she'd said goodbye and hung up the phone. After all, these were the people she still considered reasonable suspects in the deaths of her parents and the crash that had landed her brother in the hospital for a couple of days.

Doyle would probably chew her out for not calling him for backup, but she'd seen how tired and pale he was at the office. He'd talked his way out of the hospital earlier than was probably wise, and the last thing she was going to do was tell him where she was going and what she was doing. He'd probably grab his crutches and try to follow her up the mountain, a bad idea on every conceivable level. And even if, by some miracle, he proved himself levelheaded enough to stay put and let her handle the meeting, he'd worry himself sick waiting to hear back from her.

No, she'd wait until after the meeting to tell Doyle what she'd learned. But she didn't plan to go up that mountain without some sort of backup.

She dialed Nix's number, hoping she wasn't catching him at a bad time, and growled a soft curse when the call went straight to his voice mail. "Nix, it's Dana. I've just received a call from Pete Sutherland. He's set up a meeting between me and the Hales up on Copperhead Ridge. I have to be there at four—if you get this message before then, please call me. And for heaven's sake, don't tell Doyle. He'll want to limp up here or something. Listen, they don't want me bringing anyone to the cabin with me—suspicious, I know, but I can't let this opportunity go by without giving it a shot. But I sure could use someone to watch my back from down in the parking lot—"

The message beeped, cutting her off. She considered calling back, but a glance at her watch nixed that idea. It was already three-thirty, and she had a hike up the mountain ahead of her. She'd call him one more time from the mountain with more details.

NIX PULLED OUT his phone as soon as he got back in the Ford. He had a lot of new information for Dana and the chief, thanks to his talk with Alvin Pitts, and at least one solid new avenue for investigation.

Dana's phone went straight to voice mail, so he tried the office. Ellen Flatley, the chief's assistant, informed him that Chief Massey had left for the afternoon, at his fiancée's insistence. "Can Captain Parsons help you?" she asked with prim officiousness, even though he'd known her since he was a gap-toothed kid on the Bitterwood P.D.–sponsored community baseball team. She'd been a tough third-base coach, but she'd never come to a game without a pocket full of bubble gum.

"I really need to talk to the chief, Mrs. F. Are you sure he went home?"

"He was with Ms. Hanvey, so I can't assure you of anything at all," she said with a hint of humor in her otherwise steely voice. "I can forward a message to his cell phone if you wish."

"Not necessary. I have his number. Thanks anyway." He wasn't happy about disturbing the chief now that Laney had apparently coaxed him out of the office to rest, to tell the truth. The man had looked a little pale and shaky at the office, and all the information Dana had imparted must have felt like body blows.

But his condition was a result of foul play, and Nix's meeting with Alvin Pitts might have put the investigation a lot closer to a resolution. The chief needed to know the truth.

He had started to hit the contact button to speed-dial the chief when he spotted a missed call. It was Dana's cell number—she must have called back while he was on the phone with Mrs.

Flatley. She'd left a message, he saw, but he didn't waste time checking it. He needed to talk to her anyway; might as well receive her message in person.

But when he called her number, it went straight to voice mail again. Probably on the phone with her brother, he thought, or maybe even checking in at her office. He left a quick message and hung up to call the chief.

Doyle answered on the second ring. "Nix, I can't talk—"

The alarm in the chief's voice set Nix's nerves jangling. "What's wrong?"

"I just called Dana to tell her I was heading home. She practically hung up on me."

Nix frowned. "I take it she doesn't cut you off that way normally?"

"Actually," Doyle said with obvious reluctance, "sometimes she does. When she's at work or in the middle of something important. But after the talk we just had—just trust me. Something isn't right."

"Where is she?" Nix asked, suddenly wishing he'd taken a second to listen to the voice mail she'd left him.

"I don't know. It sounded like she was in her car."

When he'd left to talk to Pitts, she hadn't told him about any plans away from the police station. He'd figured she'd wait to hear what he had to tell them before she wandered off anywhere. "Look," he told Doyle, "I missed a call from her a few minutes ago, but she left a voice mail. I'll check it and get back to you if there's anything to worry about."

"Thanks." Doyle hung up.

Nix punched in the voice-mail code and listened, with growing alarm, as Dana told him about the call from Pete Sutherland. By the time her message cut off, he had already pulled a U-turn, heading for Edgewood Road and the turnoff to Copperhead Ridge.

He tried Dana's cell phone again. This time, she answered on the second ring. "Nix, you got my message?"

"Don't go up there alone, Dana." He bit back the urge to shout at the slow-moving pickup truck lumbering up Edgewood Road in front of him. "I heard something from Alvin Pitts you need to know."

"If you're going to tell me the Hales are prime suspects in what happened to my parents, I know that already. I'm armed and I'm going to be cautious."

"Dana, there are no private cabins on Copperhead Ridge."

She was silent for a moment on the other end of the line. Finally, she spoke softly. "Are you sure?"

"Positive. The county owns and maintains the trail and environs. The only cabins on that mountain are historic sites."

Dana muttered a soft profanity. "Okay. I'm heading back—" Her voice cut off suddenly. Almost simultaneously, Nix heard a sharp crack come across the line.

"Dana?" His voice rose in fear.

"I'm under fire," she whispered urgently.

THE SECOND BULLET passed close enough that she heard the whistle of wind past her ear almost simultaneously with the report of the rifle. Clutching the cell phone with one hand, she threw herself into a thicket to her right and scrabbled for the Glock secured in the pancake holster behind her back.

She could hear Nix saying her name, the sound distant and tinny. She carefully lifted the phone back to her ear, not wanting to make any sudden moves that might betray her position to the shooter. "I'm here," she whispered.

"Are you hidden?" he asked, his voice tight with urgency.

"For the moment."

"I'm nearly at the parking area. Stay where you are. I'll come get you."

"You'll be a target if you do," she warned.

Another gunshot sounded. Close by, though it seemed to be aimed in the wrong direction.

"I don't think he sees me, but he's still shooting," she whispered, trying to will her thundering pulse to a slower, steadier beat. She needed to focus, to keep her head. *Nerves of steel, Massey. Nerves of steel.*

"Any idea of the weapon?" On Nix's end of the line, the motor noise died away. Apparently he'd reached the parking lot.

"Rifle. I didn't get a visual of the shooter, which probably means he's not that close. I don't think a pistol round would have gotten nearly as close at such a distance." She tried to remember the way the shots had sounded. "I'd say a .223 round. Nothing any bigger than that."

"Maybe a hunting rifle?"

"Maybe. Not a pistol, definitely not a shotgun." She knew that moving at this point was a very bad idea, but sitting still wasn't her style. She didn't plan to cower here like a scared little rabbit waiting for the shooter to figure out where she'd gone, and she sure as hell wasn't going to let Nix come running up the mountain into the line of fire. "Nix, stay put. I'm coming down to you."

"Hell, no, you're not. I know these mountains a lot better than you do. *You* stay put. Hold on a sec—I'm going to call for backup." After a burst of static, she heard Nix calling the dispatcher, giving his location and reporting gunfire and a civilian in jeopardy. Then came the slam of a door and the sound of running footsteps.

Nix was already on the move, she realized with dismay. "Damn it, Nix, don't be stupid! He has a rifle!"

"I know what I'm doing!"

She edged a little to her left, where the limbs of one of the bushes giving her cover thinned out enough for her to get a glimpse of the trail. She stretched as far into the open as she dared, looking for any sign of her attacker.

A flash of movement up the trail barely gave her time to dive back behind the thicket before another shot rang out, blasting through the leaves about a foot and a half to her left.

A muted sound came through her phone. She put the phone to her ear and heard Nix whispering her name. He sounded scared, she realized.

He was scared for her. Just as scared as she was for him.

"I've got to move," she whispered, already scooting to her right, where the bushes ended near a thick-trunked pine tree. "He's spotted me."

"Be careful!" His voice came out breathless, and she realized he was moving again. But if he was coming up the trail behind her, he wasn't making any noise. *The man must be part moun-*

tain goat, she thought, and she felt a flutter in her chest that seemed curiously more like girlish adoration than fear. If she weren't hiding from a crazy gunman, she might have laughed.

Could she have picked a more inopportune moment to figure out she was already more than halfway in love with Walker Nix?

"I have to pocket the phone," she whispered as she prepared to cross the open space between the thicket and the tree. She shoved her phone in the pocket of her jeans, gathered herself for a quick leap and jumped.

The shot came, as anticipated, but a second too late. It ripped through the bush she'd just left behind after she was already safely behind the tree.

She let her heartbeat settle and looked for her next hiding place if the shooter started to get too close. At least if she kept moving, she might draw the sniper into the open, luring him close enough to draw a bead on him with her pistol.

What she wouldn't give for a rifle right now, she thought.

She pulled her cell phone from her pocket, hoping she hadn't cut Nix off. "Nix?" she whispered into the receiver.

There was no answer.

"Nix!" she whispered more urgently.

Suddenly, from up the trail, she heard Nix's voice call out, "Bitterwood Police! Drop your weapon."

For a taut second, his voice echoed through the trees. Then another rifle shot rang out, followed quickly by the hard concussion of a bigger round. She felt as if her heart had stopped for one long, electrifying moment.

He shot Nix, she thought, and the world seemed to fall away beneath her feet, leaving her spinning helplessly in a cold, dark place.

Then all hell broke loose in the woods just forty yards in front of her.

Chapter Sixteen

The shooter moved more quickly than Nix was expecting, crashing laterally through the dense spring undergrowth and weaving in and out of the trees. A light breeze blew from the west, shaking the trees and bushes, giving the camouflage-clad man with a rifle cover to blend in.

A sudden flurry of movement about forty yards down the trail drew Nix's attention away from the fleeing suspect, and he swung his Colt 1911 toward the commotion until he spotted sunlight glancing off a tangle of auburn hair. Dana, he realized, altering his aim so she was no longer in his sights.

She whirled to face him, her gun lifting, and he realized that the camouflage jacket and cap he'd donned to mask his approach might be working against him. He called her name, and she lowered the Glock, bending at the waist.

He tried to spot the shooter again, but he couldn't see anyone in the woods ahead. Dropping his gaze to the trail where he'd last seen the man, he spotted several large, red patches. Crouching for a better look, he saw the blotches were still wet where the liquid hadn't seeped into the dry ground.

Blood. The round from his Colt must have hit the sniper.

As he stood again, peering through the woods for any sign of movement, Dana jogged up the trail toward him, keeping low, letting the trees and undergrowth give her cover.

"Do you see him?" she asked as she drew near.

He shook his head. "He's in full camo. He could be anywhere."

Dana's hand closed over his arm in a tight grip, drawing his attention away from the woods and back to her. Her green eyes reflected the cooler hues of the forest, and in them he saw the first welling of tears.

He caught her arms and pulled her to face him, instantly alarmed. "Are you hurt?"

She shook her head, tears sliding down her cheeks. "I thought he'd shot you."

Her emotional reaction caught him flat-footed. He shook his head, at a loss. "I'm fine. But there's blood on the trail. I think my round hit him."

She let go of his arm and knuckled away the moisture on her face, nodding. "Maybe the blood trail will lead us to him."

They found dozens of blood splotches as they followed a southwesterly path through the woods off Copperhead Trail, but apparently the shooter hadn't been injured badly enough that the wound had slowed his escape.

"What's in this direction?" Dana asked.

"Over the hill is Edgewood Road, which can take him back to town or west to Maryville. From there, he could go almost anywhere."

An engine roared suddenly to life, sending birds fluttering up from the trees about a hundred yards dead ahead. Nix started running toward the sound, Dana's footsteps close behind.

"Is that an ATV?" Dana asked breathlessly.

"Has to be." Nix picked up speed as he headed in the direction of the noise. Other than a horse, only an all-terrain vehicle would be of any use this far up the mountain.

But trying to follow the noise proved futile; there was no way they could make up any ground on the ATV on foot. As the sound faded into the distance, Nix pulled up and bent at the waist to catch his breath.

Dana stopped beside him, breathing hard and looking angry. "*Now* backup finally arrives."

He heard the sirens then, growing closer. Wrapping his arm around her shoulders, he hugged her close, pressing his nose into her hair and breathing deeply. She smelled good. Hot and sweet and uniquely Dana.

And he'd come so damned close to losing her out here in these woods.

Her arms curling around his waist, she flattened herself against him, rubbing her cheek against his shoulder. "Are you sure you're not hurt?"

"I'm fine." He dropped a kiss against her temple. "Are you positive you're not hurt? Adrenaline might mask an injury at first—"

She lifted her face to look at him. "I'm fine. Pissed, but fine."

He forced his mind away from how good she felt in his arms to focus on what had just happened and what they should do next. "How sure are you that it was really Pete Sutherland on the phone with you this afternoon?"

He saw her give the question a moment of thought before her eyes met his, blazing emerald-green. "About ninety percent," she said finally. "I've met him just the one time, but we had a long conversation. And in my line of work, you learn to get pretty good at recognizing voices. It's part of how you identify perps sometimes—being able to pick out a voice in a crowd."

"Okay, then." Keeping his arm draped over her shoulders, he started walking back toward the hiking trail. "I guess we know what to do next."

"Go see Pete Sutherland?"

He gave her shoulders a squeeze. "Let's see what the old man has to say for himself."

SUTHERLAND ENTERPRISES WASN'T the high-powered media corporation it had been twenty years earlier, but apparently the fruits of their long run of success hadn't been squandered during the lean years, for the two-story neoclassical dwelling on Main Street that housed the *Bitterwood Town Crier* and the Sutherland Enterprises corporate offices reeked of money, from the spotlessly clean exterior to the rich Persian rugs adorning the highly polished maple-wood floor in the foyer.

To Dana's relief, Nix didn't bother with any small-town polite chat when he spoke to the well-dressed young woman manning the reception desk. He simply flashed his badge, told her if she announced his arrival to anyone in the building he'd charge her with obstruction and started up the stairs to the second floor, taking them two at a time.

Dana jogged to keep up, barely tamping down a giddy grin of admiration. As a woman of action herself, she rather enjoyed watching a take-charge man doing what he did best.

Some of her giddiness faded, however, when she realized the case might be resolved in a matter of minutes, and she'd soon be packing her bags and heading back to Atlanta.

How the hell was she going to be able to leave Nix behind? Was it even possible anymore?

Don't think about it, she told herself sternly, dragging her gaze away from Nix's broad shoulders and focusing instead on the long corridor between them and Pete Sutherland's office at the end of the hall.

The floors up here were also polished maple, gleaming in the late-afternoon light pouring through a window at the far end of the hall. Dana didn't spot any signs of blood, but the man on the ATV had gotten a big head start on wherever he was going. If he'd come here, he might have had time to clean up after himself.

Nix opened the door to Sutherland's office without knocking and led the way in. From his desk chair, Pete Sutherland looked up at them with benign curiosity, rising to his feet with courtly politeness. "What a nice surprise! What brings you here this afternoon, Miss Massey? And Walker Nix. Always a pleasure—"

"I was quite surprised to learn, Mr. Sutherland, that there are no privately owned cabins on Copperhead Ridge." Dana took a couple of steps forward until she was right in front of the desk, towering over Sutherland, who leaned his head back to meet her angry gaze.

He blinked in apparent confusion. "Who on earth told you there were?"

"You did," she answered. "Earlier this afternoon when you called my cell phone and sent me into an ambush."

Sutherland was good, she thought as she watched his face twist with concern. "An ambush? Good Lord, how frightening!"

"She didn't even get to the first trail shelter before a man in camo took shots at her," Nix growled. Dana spared him a glance, finding him standing close by, as if ready to pounce at the first sign of trouble. His expression was darkly grim and forbidding.

She wouldn't want to be Pete Sutherland right now, she thought, returning her gaze to the old man's face.

Sutherland pulled his glasses off and folded them carefully before setting them on the desk in front of him. He looked up at Nix. "I assume you're investigating the situation, Officer?"

Nix's smile looked downright feral. "Detective. And yes, I am investigating, Mr. Sutherland. For instance, right now my chief of detectives is speaking to Judge Garvey about a warrant to check your phone records to establish that you were, indeed, the person who called Deputy Marshal Massey and lured her into an ambush by promising her a meeting with your daughter and son-in-law."

"I had no idea she wanted such a meeting." Sutherland turned his attention from Nix to Dana, his expression softening. "You should have come to me, my dear. I would have gladly asked Nina and Paul to speak with you."

"I'll keep that in mind."

"But until you come up with your warrant— and I should warn you that my dear friend Judge Garvey is not a man who easily agrees to an invasion of an innocent man's privacy for frivolous reasons—I must ask you to go now. I have work to do."

Great, Dana thought, looking away in disgust. The judge was a friend. In a place this small, of course he was.

As her gaze glanced across a closed door behind Sutherland's desk, something on the floor just beneath the bottom of the door caught her attention. There was a small spot there, only partially visible on the light maple flooring. It glistened dark red where the overhead light hit it.

Blood, she thought, glancing at Nix.

Though he was glaring at Sutherland, who'd pointedly turned back to reading the papers on the desk in front of him, Nix must have felt her gaze on him, for he slanted a quick look at her. His eyebrows ticked upward as he apparently read the sudden excitement in her face. She glanced at the spot on the floor, then back at him. He followed her gaze and gave a slow, almost imperceptible nod.

"We could solve this whole thing if you'd just show me your phone." Nix moved around the desk toward the two wooden file cabinets that stood near the window, drawing Sutherland's gaze in that direction.

As the older man's back turned away from Dana, she pulled her Glock and hurried to the other door, whipping it open to find a walk-in closet, with shelves on the walls that held paper, boxes and supplies of all sorts.

And huddled in the center of the closet floor sat a man dressed head to toe in camouflage, from his dun-colored boots to the cap with earflaps that now hid most of his face from view.

The only bright color in that sea of drab and dun was a wet, red patch of blood soaking the man's left shoulder and upper arm.

As Dana scanned the closet for the rifle without spotting it, the man lifted his head and met her gaze, pain glazing his dark eyes.

Behind her, Nix released a soft profanity.

"Who is he?" Dana asked, not yet pointing the Glock at the man in the closet but keeping it ready, just in case.

"His name is Paul Hale." Pete Sutherland's

voice sounded about a decade older than it had only moments previously. Dana glanced his way and saw his gaze focused with dark anger on the bleeding man. "My failure of a son-in-law."

"HE'S GOING TO try to make this whole thing out to be my fault." Paul Hale's fingers trembled around the cup of water Nix had brought him, his gaze wandering around the small interview-room table but never settling on any one thing. The slug from Nix's Colt had proved easy to extract, and all the emergency-room doctor had done, once the bullet was gone, was patch up the bloody hole in the muscle. Hale wouldn't be playing golf with that arm any time soon, but, considering the trouble he was in, his golf game was the least of his worries.

"By 'he' I take it you mean your father-in-law?" Antoine Parsons, Bitterwood P.D. chief of detectives, was actually younger than Nix, though he'd put in over fifteen years with the police department now, seven of those as a detective. Doyle Massey had taken a chance on Antoine for the top detective job on the advice of his fellow detectives, who all spoke highly of the man as both a detective and a person of integrity.

Plus, Nix had conceded when the chief tapped Antoine to lead the interrogation of Paul Hale, the new chief of detectives was a virtuoso at knowing what buttons to push and when to push them to bring out the truth from a suspect.

"He's the one who did it, you know," Paul Hale muttered.

"Many things were done," Antoine said smoothly. "Which things in particular should we lay at your father-in-law's feet?"

"I didn't even know he did it. Not at that time." Paul's eyes filled with tears, his lips pressing to a thin line as he seemed to struggle with a painful emotion. Nix, who'd heard a .223 round whistle past his ear, wasn't inclined to muster up any sympathy, which was probably why Antoine was leading the interview instead of him.

"Not at what time?" Antoine asked, his voice as gentle as a mother's.

Paul Hale started to cry. "At the time my son died."

DANA LEANED HER head against Doyle's shoulder, watching the interview through the camera feed streaming into her brother's computer. "So, that's that, huh?"

"We have another brother." Doyle sounded shocked, even though all the evidence had been pointing in that direction for a few hours now. Dana didn't know how she felt herself. Not shocked, really—she'd known the minute she looked into Dalton Hale's eyes and saw echoes of her mother that he must be the child her mother had given birth to almost thirty-seven years ago.

But what came next? Dalton Hale still thought he was the son of Paul and Nina Hale. He had no idea his father was sitting in the interview room at the Bitterwood P.D. or that his grandfather was cooling his heels in a jail cell.

He wasn't going to be happy to learn he was the son of a dead woman. Or that his brother was holding the only father he'd ever known on a charge of attempted murder and his grandfather on conspiracy to attempt murder.

On the video feed, Nix reached across the table and handed Paul Hale what looked like a tissue. Hale took it and wiped his eyes. "We'd been trying to have a baby for four years, ever since we got married," he said. "The doctors kept telling us it was a long shot, but Nina couldn't bear the thought of not having a child of her own. I told her we could adopt. We'd have loved him anyway." Paul Hale wiped his eyes again. "I did love him, you know. Even after I found out. He's my son."

"You didn't know your own son had died?"

"No, of course not."

"You didn't notice the baby looked different?"

"He was a baby. He was bald and squirmy and red." Paul's laugh was a watery, desperate sound.

"To tell the truth, I was scared of him. Afraid I'd drop him and break him."

"That poor man," Dana murmured.

"That poor man tried to kill you this afternoon." Doyle's voice was hard and unsympathetic.

"This is a complicated situation, Doyle. And when Dalton finds out, it's going to get a lot messier." She gave him a stern look, one she'd been giving him off and on since they were kids. "Have a little compassion. Desperate people do desperate things."

"I'll think about it," Doyle grumbled, turning up the audio on the interview-room feed.

"Did you wonder if Tallie Cumberland might have been telling the truth about your son?" Antoine Parsons asked in a low, quiet tone. He had a good interview style, Dana thought. Lulling Hale into a sense of security, letting him think the chief of detectives might be on his side.

"Is anyone interviewing Pete Sutherland?" she asked Doyle.

"He's already asked for a lawyer. Hale didn't. He seems eager to talk."

"She was an unmarried hillbilly kid who'd just stolen our baby right out of his bassinet," Paul Hale said on the video feed, his voice rising with indignation. "Why on earth would we believe a thing she said?"

"When did you find out the truth?"

Hale went quiet for a long moment, his gaze dropping to the cup cradled between his twitching hands.

"Did your father-in-law tell you what he'd done?" Nix asked.

Hale looked up at Nix. "Not until I asked him."

"And when was that?" Antoine asked.

Hale pressed trembling fingers to his temple. "When Tallie Cumberland and her husband came to town fifteen years ago. She told me she'd left town all those years ago because she'd seen Nina and Dalton at the park. She said she realized it didn't matter whether or not he was her son by birth—he'd grown up with us and that made him ours."

Doyle slipped his arm around Dana's shoulders. She leaned her head against him again. "That sounds just like her, doesn't it?" she asked.

"Just like her," he agreed.

"Then she showed me a picture of her and her kids. Three of them. They were all nearly grown, except the youngest. She said his name was David. And God help me, I saw that boy and it was like looking at Dalton at his age. Same color hair, same face, same eyes." Hale pressed his fingers against his mouth as if he felt sick. "I knew she was right. We had her son. We'd had him all those years and never knew it."

"Does your wife know?" Antoine asked gently.

Hale shook his head. "No. I never told her."

"But you confronted your father-in-law?" Nix asked.

Hale nodded. "I knew it had to be him. He'd do anything for Nina. And he'd stayed with Nina and the baby when I left the hospital that day to go buy some things we needed for the nursery." He closed his eyes, the trembling of his lips visible even on the grainy video feed. "Our son died while Nina was napping. Pete noticed he wasn't moving, and when he checked, the baby had already turned cold. They'd thought he was sleeping."

"Mr. Sutherland didn't try to find a doctor?"

"He took the baby and tried to find a nurse, but there was an emergency situation in one of the delivery rooms down the hall and there was no one at the desk. So he went to the room down the hall, hoping he might find a nurse there. But there was only that little girl, asleep in her bed, and her little baby squirming like a worm in his bassinet."

"Oh, God," Dana murmured.

"He said he knew the girl—Tallie had worked for the newspaper awhile, helping out in the stockroom before she got pregnant. He knew she was penniless and couldn't take care of the child, and maybe if her baby was dead, she'd end up thinking it was a blessing, in a way, not to have to worry about how to feed him and take care of him."

"So he put the dead baby in the bassinet and took the live one?" Antoine asked.

Hale nodded. "I confronted him after seeing that picture of Tallie's kids. I threatened to go to Nina unless he told me the truth."

"What did he do after that?" Nix asked. Dana could tell he was angry but trying to keep his tone calm and nonconfrontational. Funny, she thought, how incredibly familiar he seemed to her, despite how short a time she'd known him. She couldn't remember the last time she'd connected with another person so quickly or deeply.

And now, just when she'd found him, it was nearly time for her to leave again. Back to Atlanta and a life that was nothing but work and sleep, day after day after day....

"I thought he understood she wasn't going to make waves. But he got so quiet after our talk. So very quiet." Hale lowered his head. "The next day, I heard about the car crash, and I knew."

"What did you know?" Nix asked.

Paul Hale lifted his gaze, his jaw squaring. "Did you know that Pete owns half interest in Brantley's Garage?"

This is it, Dana thought. *Just spit it out, for God's sake.*

"Pete loves to work on cars. It's been a hobby since he was a kid, and he still keeps his hand in things at the garage. Gets a kick out of putting on the coveralls and getting his hands greasy."

"You're saying you think he tampered with the Masseys' car?" Antoine asked, his tone carefully neutral.

Hale shook his head. "I'm saying I know he did."

Chapter Seventeen

"He wants full immunity to testify against Pete Sutherland," Antoine Parsons told Doyle Massey a half hour later. He and Nix had joined the chief in his office a few minutes earlier, after taking a break from the interview to let Paul Hale regain his composure. Dana was there as well, perched on a low bookshelf that sat beneath the window. The sun had set almost an hour ago, and the last inky light of day had nearly fled the sky outside the police station.

"He shot at Dana, Chief." Nix shook his head, not willing to consider the idea of letting Hale get away with what he'd done in the woods that afternoon. He looked over at Dana. She gazed back at him, her green eyes murky with thoughts he couldn't quite discern. He forced his gaze back to the chief. "Hale was damned lucky he's not a good shot."

"I know what he did," Massey said with a

pointed look at Nix. "I agree he shouldn't get away with the attempted murder of either of you."

"If you want to convince a jury that a well-loved citizen of this town like Pete Sutherland murdered two people in cold blood, and attempted to murder two others, then you'll need all the testimony you can get," Antoine said calmly. "I think we're going to have to give Hale something. Suspended sentence, maybe, since neither of you was hurt?"

Nix pressed his lips to a thin line to keep from arguing. If he'd been the only one Hale had shot at, maybe he'd be more willing to let it go. He'd been pointing a gun at the man, and while he didn't like the idea of leniency for people who took shots at police officers, he'd trade the charge in a minute to convict Pete Sutherland of murder.

Pete had killed Dana's parents, taken them away from her when she was barely more than a kid, and all to protect himself and his family from dealing with the truth about Dalton Hale. And Nix had a feeling, once he heard something from the state-prison warden, they might have another crime to lay at Pete Sutherland's feet.

He needed to pay.

But Hale could have killed Dana in the woods. If he'd been better with the rifle, she'd be dead. And he'd meant to kill her. Nix had no doubt.

No way could he condone letting Hale walk on that charge.

"Has Sutherland's lawyer arrived?" Antoine asked Doyle.

"A half hour ago. I'm expecting—"

The door to the chief's office opened suddenly, and Dalton Hale strode into the room, leashed anger vibrating from every inch of his body. His green-eyed gaze scanned the room and settled on Doyle Massey, rage twisting his face. "I don't know who you think you are or what you have against my family, but I want my father and my grandfather released immediately."

Doyle pushed to his feet, bracing his hands against the desk to keep himself upright. "They've been charged with very serious crimes. I can't let them go until they've gone before a judge."

"My grandfather's lawyer tells me you're charging him with murder in the deaths of Cal and Tallie Massey—your kin, I presume?"

"Our parents." Dana stood from her perch on the bookcase.

Dalton turned to look at her. "Were you planning this the whole time we were at lunch together?"

"No," she answered.

"I want to see my father. I understand you haven't allowed him to talk to a lawyer?"

"He waived his right to a lawyer," Antoine answered, his voice calm.

His soothing style had no effect on Dalton Hale. "That's ridiculous. I demand to see him right now."

Antoine moved toward the door. "I'll ask if he'll speak to you."

Nix wanted to protest, not willing to watch his best hope of seeing Pete Sutherland pay for his crimes swept away by a change of heart. But they could mess up the case in a big way by not allowing the suspects to invoke their Fifth Amendment rights.

They'd have to take a chance.

The silence that fell across the room after Antoine left was thick with tension, not all of it coming from Dalton Hale. Dana's face was pale, her expression strained as her gaze lingered on the face of the half brother she'd never known. What was she thinking? This reunion couldn't be turning out the way she would have wanted. Nix wanted to cross the room and put his arms around her, to reassure her that whatever happened next, he was there for her. He'd support her in anything she chose to do next.

Anything, that was, but leaving him behind.

He didn't think he could ask her to stick around Bitterwood, so he was going to have to leave the mountains again. He'd survived much harsher places than Atlanta. He wasn't much for city life, but he'd adapt. As long as she let him be part of her life, he'd go anywhere she wanted.

But was that what *she* wanted?

Antoine came back into the room. "Your father will see you."

Nix glanced at Dana. She was looking at Dalton, her eyes dark with concern. She was worried about him, he realized, about what he might be on the verge of discovering about his life. Forget her own pain, her own sense of having her life turned upside down. She was worried about her brother.

The door closed behind Dalton and Antoine, leaving Nix alone in the room with Dana and her brother. Doyle released a long, pent-up breath and dropped heavily into his chair.

"You don't have to stick around for the rest of this, Nix," he said with a weary grimace. "It's been a long day for you. Go home. Get some rest."

Nix looked at Dana. She was watching him with a sober expression that made his chest ache. "Can I give you a ride home?" he asked.

She shook her head. "I need to stick around. I'm not sure what Hale's going to tell Dalton, and I don't want to leave Doyle here to take the brunt of his reaction."

"I don't need protecting," Doyle protested.

Her answer was to perch herself firmly on the bookcase again.

"Why don't I run down to the diner and get us all something to eat while we're waiting?" Nix suggested. "Tonight's special is pork barbecue sandwiches."

"I'm not hungry." Dana had turned to look out the window, where the darkness was now almost complete, save for the sparkle of lights from the handful of buildings still open on Main Street.

He'd get her something anyway, he thought. In case she changed her mind. "How about you, Chief?"

"I could go for a barbecue sandwich," Doyle admitted. He dug in his pocket and pulled out his wallet. "Get one for Laney, too. She'll probably be here before you get back."

Dana stood suddenly. "I'll go with you, Nix."

He was a little surprised by the change of mind, but he wasn't going to quibble. They hadn't had a chance to talk alone since they'd brought Pete Sutherland and Paul Hale into custody. He had so many things he wanted to say to her, starting with how scared he'd been to hear those gunshots ringing through her cell phone.

He could have lost her. A few small inches had been the difference between walking through the Bitterwood police station with her by his side as he was now and holding her dying body while he tried to keep her from bleeding out.

It had been close. Too damned close. And even though she'd shown her own emotions when she'd touched his face and let him know how worried she'd been about him, he hadn't told her about his own fears.

Between life in the marine corps and life as a cop, he'd gotten used to keeping his feelings carefully hidden, sublimating them behind the job that had to be done.

But if he wanted to be part of Dana's life, he needed to tell her. Even if she ended up telling him she didn't want the same thing he did, he still had to tell her how he felt.

He should have told her before now. Should have made her understand how important she was to him, how unwilling he was to let her walk out of his life.

But before he could muster up the elusive words, she asked, "Do you think Paul Hale will tell Dalton the truth?"

"If he wants a deal, he'll have to come clean." Nix flattened his hand between her shoulder blades as they headed down the corridor past the interview rooms. She edged closer until their bodies almost bumped as they walked.

That was a good sign, wasn't it?

Dana released a quiet huff of breath. "This really isn't how I wanted things to go with Dalton."

"I know."

"Doyle and I weren't even sure we wanted to tell him, after all this time. It's not like we expect him to welcome a new brother and sister with open arms or anything. I mean, we wouldn't have liked letting the Hales get away with stealing him from our mother, but she'd made her peace with letting him stay with the Hales, right?"

"That's what Alvin said, and I don't see any reason to doubt him."

"But now letting things slide is no longer an option."

As they neared the door of the third interview room, it opened and Dalton Hale burst into the hallway, his whole body vibrating with anger. He nearly ran straight into Dana and pulled up quickly, his upper lip curling as he looked at her.

"You're not my sister."

Nix felt the briefest of trembles dart up Dana's back, then her spine hardened and her chin lifted as she spoke. "You've spoken to your father."

"That's right. *My father.*" Dalton emphasized the last two words, his jaw so tight the words came out in a growl. But almost as soon as the words died away in the space between them, his whole body seemed to sag as if someone had pulled out a stopper and let all of the air out of him. "He's not a bad man. Neither is my grand-father. They shouldn't be in jail."

Nix kept his thoughts on the subject to himself, not so much for Hale's benefit as for Dana's. She hadn't come to Bitterwood to hurt anyone, least of all this man standing in front of them. But he pressed his hand more firmly to her back to let her know whose side he was on.

"This is a bad time to talk about this," Dana said with a gentleness he hadn't often heard from her. "We've all learned things about the past that have caught us flat-footed—"

"Don't try to handle me," Dalton said coldly. "If you think you can erase the harm you've done by playing the innocent—"

"That's enough," Nix said.

"It's okay," Dana said. "Mr. Hale has a right to be upset."

"Not with you," Nix disagreed. He looked at Hale, who was looking at them through narrowed eyes. "You know, I get that you've just been smacked in the face by the emotional equivalent of a two-by-four, Dalton. And I'm real sorry about that. You sure as hell didn't do anything to deserve it. But the way you're acting now is out of bounds, and if you can't keep a civil tongue in your head while you sort out your mess, then I think you'd better steer clear of Dana and her brother for a while."

"Nix—"

"This isn't over." Dalton straightened his tie and glanced back toward the interview-room door, which had closed behind him. "I'm going to look at everything you did today in bringing in my father and my grandfather. I'm going to examine every statement, every sideways look, every possible angle by which you could have screwed up. And if I find any breach, anything at all, I will use it. And I'll make sure everyone in this town knows exactly whom they hired for their chief of police and whom he's chosen to work for him." His gaze swung from Nix's face to Dana's. His eyes hardened to chips of green ice. "Your brother has made the wrong enemies. He's going to pay for it."

He turned and walked down the hallway toward the exit.

Dana stood very still for a long moment. Then she sagged against the wall, covering her face with her hands. "That went well," she murmured from beneath her palms.

Nix gently tugged her hands away from her face. "Are you okay?"

She looked as if she wanted to cry, the muscles of her face twitching in an effort to restrain the urge. "Yeah. I'm okay. It's just—" She looked down the hall toward the exit, as if she could catch a glimpse of Dalton's back. "You have no idea how much he looks like David. And standing here, with him staring at me with so much anger and disgust—" She wrapped her arms around her stomach, shaking her head. "It just got to me."

Nix wrapped his arms around her shoulders, tugging her into his embrace. "He's going to come around."

"I'm not so sure," she murmured, pressing her cheek to his. "But thanks for standing up for me."

"Always."

She tilted her head back, looking up at his face. The hint of a smile curved her mouth. "Don't suppose I could hire you to come back to Atlanta with me and go around telling people off on my behalf?"

"I'd come for free," he said, his tone serious.

Her faint smile faded. "You'd leave here and come to Atlanta with me? Really?"

"If that's what you wanted."

She stared at him a moment, her eyes soft and thoughtful. "I don't want you to come to Atlanta."

Dismay jolted through him, settling like an ache in the center of his chest. He released her and started to step back. "Oh."

She flattened her hand against his chest swiftly. "Wait, don't look at me like that." She curled her fingers, gathering a fistful of his shirt to pull him back toward her. "I'm not brushing you off. I'm just saying 'no' to going back to Atlanta."

"I don't think I have what it takes for a long-distance relationship."

"Oh, God, me neither," she said quickly. "Nix, I don't want to go back there, either. I want to stay here. My brother's here. My soon-to-be sister-in-law. And yeah, even Dalton. Maybe he'll never change his mind about us, but that doesn't mean I don't want to try to get to know him." She loosened her grip on him, sliding her hand up his chest to wrap her fingers around the back of his neck. "And you're here."

"I am," he agreed, the ache in his chest transforming into a bright warmth that flooded his whole body with a sense of relief.

"Do you think we're crazy?" she asked, stepping closer. "I mean, we met only a few days ago."

"It's fast," he agreed. "But I know we fit together. Don't you?"

"Yeah." The shaky smile she flashed at him rocked his nervous system like a jolt of lightning. His skin felt tingly and full of energy, and the urge to pick her up and whirl her around almost overcame his good sense. He settled for a swift kiss that trembled just on the verge of something a whole lot deeper and hotter.

He dragged his mouth away from hers and smiled. "Just so we're clear, we're talking about the future, not just now."

Her brow furrowed with sudden concern. "You mean, like, marriage and forever and all that?"

Uh-oh. "Yeah. Is that a problem?"

She stared at him for a long moment, her expression betraying dismay. Then the wrinkles in her brow disappeared in a flash, and she shot him another one of those tingle-inducing grins. "You're such a sucker. I'm going to have to remember that. Could come in handy."

"You're evil," he said with a growl, tugging her back into his arms. "Good thing I like a woman with a wicked streak."

She nodded toward the exit. "Come on. Let's go to the diner before Doyle and his crutches come looking for us."

LANEY HANVEY ARRIVED as Dana and Nix were returning to the police station with bags of food for their dinner. Apparently Doyle had caught her up on the events of the day by phone, because she gave Dana an impulsive hug and told her how glad she was that Dana was okay. "I can't believe Paul Hale tried to shoot you."

"Believe it," Nix growled.

Dana slid her hand behind his back, giving him a soothing caress between his shoulder blades.

"He was a terrible shot. I sort of wonder if he missed on purpose. It was Pete Sutherland who put him up to it."

"And that's even more of a shock." Laney shook her head. "Old Pete is like a town fixture. I have no idea what people around here are going to think of all this."

"I don't imagine it's going to be easy for Doyle." Dana sighed. Her brother had already dealt with a number of problems in his short tenure as Bitterwood's chief of police. Having one of the most well-respected families in town pitted against him couldn't help.

"He's tough. He can handle it," Laney said with such loving confidence, Dana couldn't help smiling. Her brother had lucked out coming to Bitterwood, she thought.

Just as she had.

She glanced at Nix and saw him looking at her with all sorts of delicious promises in his dark eyes. Despite her earlier insistence that she stick around to watch her brother's back, she now found herself wondering how quickly she and Nix could make their excuses to leave the station and head to Nix's little cabin in the woods.

I'm a terrible sister, she thought as she followed Laney into her brother's office.

No, contradicted a quiet little voice in the back of her mind. *You're a woman in love.*

"The D.A. has already called wanting a full accounting of the arrests," Doyle told Nix as soon as he kissed Laney hello. "I hate to ask you to stick around longer tonight, but I need your report on my desk first thing in the morning."

"Doyle—" Dana began.

Nix put his hand on her shoulder. "He's right. We need this thing stitched up good and tight. I'll get to work on it after dinner."

Doyle's gaze settled on Nix's hand on Dana's shoulder. One sandy eyebrow lifted in surprise, and his green-eyed gaze flashed her way.

Might as well tell him what she'd decided, she thought. "I'm staying in Bitterwood."

Doyle's eyes narrowed. "Until the wedding?"

"For good."

His gaze slid to Nix's face briefly before returning to lock with hers. "What about your job?"

"I've been in Atlanta for five years. I can ask for a transfer to Knoxville. If there's an opening, they'll accommodate me."

"And if there's not an opening?"

"Then I'll get another job."

Doyle gave her a long, considering look. "If you're thinking you're going to be able to have some sort of happy, shiny relationship with Dalton Hale—"

"I have no illusions about that," she assured him. She glanced at Nix, and he smiled his encouragement. "But I still have you. And Laney now."

"And my newest detective?"

"Is that going to be a problem?" Nix asked bluntly.

Doyle held up his hands. "I'm the younger brother. She'd kick my ass if I tried to make it one."

"And you know it," Dana murmured, knowing full well that if Doyle really had a problem with it, he wouldn't let her status as the older sibling get in the way. She'd take his response as a vote of approval.

"Did you see Dalton Hale on the way out?" Doyle asked as they settled into the chairs around his desk.

"Briefly," Dana answered.

Doyle winced. "How bad was it?"

"Bad enough."

"He's not an unreasonable guy." Laney took the sandwich Dana handed her with a sympathetic smile. "He just needs time to deal with finding out a lot of his life has been a lie."

"Paul Hale says Nina doesn't have any idea Dalton's not her son," Doyle told his fiancée.

"That poor woman," Laney murmured.

"Our poor mother," Doyle answered, looking at Dana.

What must life have been like for her mother, Dana wondered, knowing all these years that she had another son, a boy she couldn't acknowledge for fear it would destroy his life?

As she settled back in silence, letting the chit-chat of the others flow around her, she wondered about her mother's decision to come back here to Bitterwood and see what had become of the boy she'd left behind. Did she get to see him, even a brief glimpse to reassure herself that her sacrifice had been worth it?

What would she think of her children now, of the hard and treacherous path that lay ahead of them if they were all three to find any sort of relationship with each other?

She'd hope for the best and prepare for the worst, Dana thought. Just as she always had, all their lives. She'd love them all and encourage them to be patient and understanding with each other.

Oh, Mama, she thought, *I haven't always followed your advice, and I've had a lot of regrets. But this time, I'll try.*

She felt Nix's attention, and she turned to find him watching her. His lips twitched with a smile.

She smiled back, feeling a sudden sense of peace about the future, as if her mother had put her arm around Dana's shoulders and whispered "I think this one's a keeper" in her ear.

Me, too, Mama, she thought, reaching across the space between them to take Nix's hand. *Me, too.*

* * * * *

Don't miss the suspenseful conclusion of
award-winning author Paula Graves's
BITTERWOOD P.D. *miniseries.*
Look for
THE LEGEND OF SMUGGLER'S CAVE
next month, wherever
Harlequin Intrigue books are sold!

LARGER-PRINT BOOKS!
GET 2 FREE LARGER-PRINT NOVELS PLUS 2 FREE GIFTS!

HARLEQUIN

INTRIGUE

BREATHTAKING ROMANTIC SUSPENSE

YES! Please send me 2 FREE LARGER-PRINT Harlequin Intrigue® novels and my 2 FREE gifts (gifts are worth about $10). After receiving them, if I don't wish to receive any more books, I can return the shipping statement marked "cancel." If I don't cancel, I will receive 6 brand-new novels every month and be billed just $5.49 per book in the U.S. or $5.99 per book in Canada. That's a saving of at least 13% off the cover price! It's quite a bargain! Shipping and handling is just 50¢ per book in the U.S. and 75¢ per book in Canada.* I understand that accepting the 2 free books and gifts places me under no obligation to buy anything. I can always return a shipment and cancel at any time. Even if I never buy another book, the two free books and gifts are mine to keep forever.

199/399 HDN F42Y

Name	(PLEASE PRINT)	
Address		Apt. #
City	State/Prov.	Zip/Postal Code

Signature (if under 18, a parent or guardian must sign)

Mail to the **Harlequin® Reader Service:**
IN U.S.A.: P.O. Box 1867, Buffalo, NY 14240-1867
IN CANADA: P.O. Box 609, Fort Erie, Ontario L2A 5X3

**Are you a subscriber to Harlequin Intrigue books
and want to receive the larger-print edition?
Call 1-800-873-8635 today or visit www.ReaderService.com.**

HILP13R

Reader Service.com

Manage your account online!

- Review your order history
- Manage your payments
- Update your address

> ### *We've designed the Harlequin® Reader Service website just for you.*

Enjoy all the features!

- Reader excerpts from any series
- Respond to mailings and special monthly offers
- Discover new series available to you
- Browse the Bonus Bucks catalog
- Share your feedback

Visit us at:
ReaderService.com